A Native American boy was talking with his grandfather. "What do you think about the world situation?" he asked. The grandfather replied, "I feel like wolves are fighting in my heart. One is full of anger and hatred; the other is full of love, forgiveness, and peace." "Which one will win?" asked the boy. To which the grandfather replied, "The one I feed." (Origin unknown)

"Where today are the Pequot? Where are the Narragansett, the Mohican, the Pokanoket, and many other once powerful tribes of our people? They have vanished before the avarice and the oppression of the white man, as snow before the summer sun." (Tecumseh)

…"I am tired of fighting. Our chiefs are killed…. The old men are all dead. It is the young men who say yes or no…. It is cold and we have no blankets. The little children are freezing to death. My people, some of them have run away to the hills and have no blankets, no food…." (Joseph)

"We did not ask you white men to come here. The Great Spirit gave us this country as a home. You had yours. We did not interfere with you…." (Crazy Horse)

"It was lonesome, the leaving. Husband dead, friends buried or held prisoners. I felt that I was leaving all that I had but I did not cry….We had done no wrong…" (Wetatonmi)

Other books by the author

Non-Fiction:

My Time—Thousands Went to Broadway,
Millions Went to Auschwitz

The Dead Road

Tasting Blood

Lady Law

Out of Control

Fiction:

Island Girl

PEOPLE OF THE HILLS

What they didn't teach you

JACK EDGERTON

Member of the WRITERS GROUP

PEOPLE OF THE HILLS
WHAT THEY DIDN'T TEACH YOU

iUniverse books may be ordered through booksellers or by contacting:

iUniverse
1663 Liberty Drive
Bloomington, IN 47403
www.iuniverse.com
844-349-9409

Cover Art by Mackenzie Edgerton

ISBN: 978-1-6632-3036-2 (sc)
ISBN: 978-1-6632-3037-9 (e)

Print information available on the last page.

iUniverse rev. date: 10/13/2021

The Good Mind offers an alternative to what happened (American Holocaust): "Don't dwell on the past, learn from it. Move on in positive ways. Find solutions to strengthen relationships."

INTRODUCTION

"For those who were here first"

It's March 11th, 2005 and an article on the front page of the *Syracuse Post Standard*, lets us know that some of the residents of the Onondaga Nation are appearing that morning in downtown Syracuse at the Federal Building to present legal papers regarding land rights.

I have a feeling that they'll want to be there early to avoid the press and a potentially hostile crowd. I placed a phone call to Sean Kirst at the paper, who wrote the article; to hopefully get more information as to the time and place of this meeting and to inquire if it would be open to the public. He said that he'd probably meet me there—he didn't show.

Knowing that I would soon be writing my next book on The People, I just had to get down there to witness "history in the making", so to speak. After a quick shower, I hastily said, "good-bye" for the day letting my wife and daughter know that this was a most serious event and something that I wanted to personally attend.

As I'm arriving at the parking lot across from the Federal Building, walking toward me is none other than Sid Hill. He is on his way to represent the Onondaga, as their leader, in their land rights issue. Sid, by the way, is the *Tadodaho* to the entire Six Nations. They call him the "Fire keeper." He is the unassuming, quiet leader in the book.

But I'm getting way ahead on this story. We need to back-up about 14,000 to 15,000 years. As I mentioned in a previous book I wrote, *"MY TIME-Thousands Went to Broadway-Millions Went to Auschwitz,"* we're going to look at these "first" people and the abhorring way they were and are being treated and *mistreated.*

I am by trade an importer-wholesaler, not a historian by any means. I disliked picking up a history book in prep school and, as I recall, American History was not one of my more popular subjects either. Who wanted to memorize all those dates? Dates in this book are for reference points relating to significant events in a sequence in the overall story of the Six Nation Confederacy. They're only here for a time frame.

I am, however, going to explore some events in greater detail than your history book ever did. Some happenings are going to be a revelation to you. I'm not going to win any popularity contest, but that's the way it goes. As Sid once said to me when I told him that I was writing a book about his people, "If it's not truthful, it's not worth telling. If it is true then don't worry about what others will say."

They say that the telling of history belongs to the victors, so do your research well.

To better understand our Amerind (American Indian) sisters and brothers, we need to go back in time to when it is said and theorized that they first inhabited this area in what is now called New York State wherein lie separate sovereign countries, the Onondaga Nation Territory being one of them.

It might surprise you to learn that they have their own laws, government, school (K-8), security, fire department, boundaries, language, flag, passport, religion, indigenous food, clothing style, culture, history and pride.

I have learned that there are disputes with other tribes and internal disagreements, as well. I probably won't go into much detail as nobody wants me to use their name in this book. I have opinions galore but no quotes that I can use.

You'll understand how they've influenced the way we live and more importantly the way we've changed their lives.

As Cavalli-Sforza wrote, "I found myself face to face with history, with the paths trodden by those few thousands or tens of thousands of people who, over a period of one hundred thousand years, colonized every corner of the earth. Native Americans numbered in the millions at one point in time but now figure in the mere thousands, some due to warfare and a great deal to the inability to fight off our diseases." (germ warfare)

"To truly know a race you must study their archeology, history, demography, linguistics, and statistics. We must remember that what unifies us outweighs what makes us different. Skin color and body shape, language and culture, are all that differentiate the peoples across the earth." (Pg. xi Cavalli-Sforza)

The research on this book will be interesting for me as well. It hopefully will eliminate some of my personal ignorance about my neighbors to the south. You see, the very first time that I was at the Onondaga Nation, I was terrified! Our family was on the way to go apple-picking on Route 20. For us, Route 11A was a shortcut through their territory. All that my dad had to mention were the words, "Indian reservation" and I couldn't wait to put the windows up in the car. Being a warm day, they all wondered why I wanted the car closed up. In my impressionable state as a very young boy I preferred not to get hit by a stray Indian arrow as we passed by, like a stagecoach. Such wrong impressions were given to the white movie audience by white producers of "B" movies—no wonder I was warped!

Years later when my suppliers from Japan came over on a business trip, one of their first requests was to see real, live, "Indians." Well, needless to say, it wasn't what they expected. They too were brought up on "B" Westerns and were looking for tee-pees as well as Natives riding around on horseback with full feather head-dress typical of the plains Indians at a gathering. Instead they got mobile homes, pick-up trucks, and baseball caps.

Ready? Come explore these fascinating people with me. We'll go from mastodon to Burger King, buckskin to Calvin Klein. Their CK brand on clothing doesn't stand for Calvin Klein; I'll let you figure it out.

CHAPTER ONE

TERMINOLOGY

When I refer to the first people that settled this area I'll try to use the words Amerind or The People, or better yet—*Haudenosaunee* pronounced 'ho-dee-no-sho-nee.' They don't like words of the whites to describe them such as "Native Americans" (for the most part they don't consider themselves Americans, so I'll respect their sovereignty); "Iroquois or *Hiroquois*" as they were labeled by the French; "Indians or *Indios*" as they were wrongly identified by Christopher Columbus; "savages" as they were branded by the early settlers and U.S. Cavalry; or "red skins" coined by the trailblazer Kit Carson in the books and movies to denote a body of individuals that, in fact, do not possess that skin color; or the use of other derogatory words that I frequently hear but I'm not going to mention. When any of the above words are used by me, they generally are in a quoted passage or used in context.

"In the Iroquois way, from the frequent use of a tinted all-natural suntan lotion that they had developed, it gave their naturally white skin a reddish-brown glow, which racists assumed (and still assume) was their natural color." (Mann pg. 101) I'm sure you remember Anthony Quinn, the Greek actor, who portrayed Indians in Saturday westerns, looking like he just stepped out of the tanning parlor.

I'm usually of darker complexion than my friends on the "rez" as I tan easily. With my skin color, grayish hair, and blue eyes, I'm assigned the name, "Mohawk Jack," by many who know me. The children on the rez quite often are curious as to what clan I belong to i.e. beaver, turtle, snipe, etc. As I'm of Scottish ancestry, I use my clan name of MacMillan which totally confuses them until I explain that we both have clan origins.

CHAPTER TWO

VERY EARLY TIMES

I 'll give you a timeline that will help to organize their story and that of neighboring tribes. It hopefully will assist you to follow the movement, lifestyle, conflicts, relations with non-Amerinds, and the many problems that they face today.

Artifacts that are discovered today reveal so much about the living conditions, diet, and technology of tools and weapons used hundreds of years ago. Most artifacts that are found consist of pottery, bone fragments, or implements made from stone. Items made years ago from skin, cloth, wood, rawhide, or organic materials used for articles such as baskets or clothing would rot and would not stand the test of time.

The abundance of articles that were found preserved in gravesites, contributed greatly to filling in the gaps about the lifestyle of the early Amerinds. True, these were sacred places and should never have been disturbed; but ignorance quite often leads to knowledge.

I heard from an archeologist at a lecture that it is now against the law to own complete and intact artifacts in New York State. They more than likely came from a burial site. This should help to prevent people from disturbing Amerind gravesites. I personally own a few that I bid on at local auctions which I'll eventually give to the *Tadodaho* for safe keeping or as a donation to the Iroquois Museum on Route 88 outside of Schenectady, NY.

13000-8000 BC The Ice Age is coming to an end. The Wisconsin Ice Shelf is starting to break up and melt making northern overland routes available (ice was as high as two miles in some areas with accompanying bitter cold). Migration in this region was mainly along the southern shore of Lake Iroquois (Lake Ontario and expanded area). Wild game and fish became plentiful and the tribes followed their food sources. The glaciers, as they had proceeded south from Canada, had carved out very deep valleys as they sliced across New York State. As the ice shelf receded and melted, the eleven Finger Lakes were formed (inlets from the south, outlets to the north).

11000-6500 BC Paleo-Indian hunters moved east between the Laurentian Upland Province (Canada) and the Glaciated Alleghany Plateau (New York) comprising the north and south shores of Lake Erie (5-10 mile corridor along the shoreline) and Lake Ontario (approx. 35 mile corridor along the southern shore, 35-40 miles along the northern shore). As soon as the ice shelf retreated to the north, the St. Lawrence River valley was open to carry the melting ice water to the northeast and eventually to the ocean thereby relieving the strain on the Mohawk River which flowed east to the Albany region and the Hudson River.

The Seneca River carrying the outflow from the Finger Lakes, now joined the Oneida River and the north-flowing Oswego River at a junction called Three Rivers which is northeast of present day Syracuse. You can readily see the importance of these water routes to the Iroquois tribes not only for food but transportation for wartime purposes, as well.

8000 BC The archeological dig site, West Athens Hill, is situated 3 miles west of the Hudson River in Greene County containing 1,400 artifacts, all Paleo-Indian. "While by far the bulk of the chipped-stone artifacts were derived from the local flint outcrops, a small remainder made of exotic flints is present, comprising Pennsylvania jasper, Ohio Upper Mercer flint, and Western New York-Onondaga flint. This fact may indicate regions in which these nomadic people had sojourned prior to their entry into the Hudson Valley. (Ritchie XV-XVI) (Onondaga flint strongly indicates a west to east movement)

Kings Road Site is 2 miles west of the Hudson River in Greene

County also containing fluted points, artifacts and chipping debris, end scrapers, side scrapers, and flake knives. Found were 351 artifacts at one site. "Of special interest is the high percentage of exotic flints on this component which utilized chiefly the local Normanskill flint. Approx. 10% of the total collection of tools was imported into the eastern New York area from regions to the west, south, and north. Recognizably.... the western variety of Onondaga flint may have come from western New York or adjacent Ontario....upper New York by Ft. Ann flint... (Ritchie XVII)

Port Mobil Site is located on the southern end of Staten Island on a location 40' above sea level (relatively undisturbed). (Ritchie XVIII)

There are more dig sites at Vergennes Site, Davis Site, and Potts Site. I don't want to bore you with a lot of technical detail so if it is of interest to you; your local library has more information. There are volumes on this topic alone.

4500-1300 BC Archaic Period (hunting-fishing-gathering)

3433 BC Lamoka Lake (this is probably one of the better dig sites situated southwest of present day Geneva, NY)

2980 BC Frontenac Island Site (Cayuga Lake) contains carbon-dated charcoal (see glossary). This is an area ½ mile from present day Union Springs. The exploration dig was on a one acre site approx. 380' above sea level. The following bones and bone fragments were found at a cook site and classified: dog (yes, they were eaten), gray wolf, black bear, raccoon, otter, bobcat, woodchuck, gray squirrel, muskrat, beaver, porcupine, Virginia deer, elk, turkey, grouse, passenger pigeon, box turtle, wood turtle, snapping turtle, northern pike, bullhead, and minor amounts of small fish and mollusks. (Ritchie pg. 107-108)

2050 BC Brewerton Site- carbon-dated charcoal (west end of Oneida Lake at Oneida River inlet). These are the bones and bone fragments and fall or early winter antlers. Based on tooth wear they were all adult animals: deer 65%, elk 15%, bear 13%, raccoon 3%, beaver 1%, (wolf, porcupine, bobcat, and turkey were less than 1%) (Information based on NYS Museum excavations in 1953—Ritchie)

1300-1000 BC Frost Island, Orient Sites (this is the Transitional period)

1000 BC-1600 AD Meadowood, Middlesex, Point Peninsula, Squawkie Hill, Lewiston Sites (this is the Woodland period)

*1142 AD Earliest date established by non-Indian scholars for the founding of the Iroquois Confederacy. (There are two other possible dates used for the founding, those being 1090 and 1451. Supposedly the Peacemaker gathered the tribes together during a total eclipse). The Peacemaker gathered representatives from the original Five Nations to bury their weapons and agree to the Great Law of Peace forming the *Haudenosaunee* Confederacy. One arrow (representing one tribe) can be broken separately but when you bind five arrows together, they can't be broken.

"...this confederacy was formed centuries before the colonists landed when five warring Iroquois tribes (Seneca, Cayuga, Oneida, Mohawk, and Onondaga) made peace and joined together in the world's first true democracy. The founding fathers of the U.S. studied this confederacy and patterned their democracy after it.

This Iroquois Confederacy was formed by the vision of the Peacemaker, a Huron Indian, and an outsider, who brought the Great Law of Peace-the law of peace and forgiveness-to the five warring tribes and established their union.

To do this, he enlisted the help of many including *Jikonsahseh* (the Peace Mother), and *Ayonwentha* (Hiawatha), an eloquent Onondaga chief ....at Long Branch Park which is the spot where The Peacemaker held the first Grand Council once all the Iroquois chiefs agreed to live in peace. It was here that the Iroquois Confederacy, the model for all future democracies, was formed.

This is sacred ground as is any place on Earth where ancient hatreds have become present loves." (www.mynewsbuilder.com pg. 1)

On a personal note, it was here at Long Branch in the summer of 2000 that I had my initial exposure to the *Haudenosaunee* culture at a "pow-wow in the park." Tribes came from all over the Northeast and Canada, and one from Mexico, for the dancing competitions, Native food, and camaraderie. It was probably one of the most peaceful events of any kind that I've ever been exposed to in my life. It was a totally drug-free and alcohol-free gathering of all different ethnic groups and ages. The music was mystical, the buffalo burger and the strawberry drink were delicious, and the Native clothing was incredible! It was an event for everyone, especially the children.

"Often the message of love and forgiveness is best received by the young who may not have yet experienced many heartbreaks [much heartbreak]. Also, many youths are being raised by electronic elders (television and pop music) which have little wisdom to impart and in many ways [faulty thinking] leads them astray." www.Roskind-mynewsletterbuilder.com pg. 2)

It was an event that taught me how to relax and to find 'peace of mind.' It had a spiritual significance to me, more so than some Sunday masses I have attended—a different way to communicate with our Creator.

The Onondaga say, "Live in peace, not in pieces." Chelsea, a daughter of ours, has adopted this philosophy in her life. She used that expression as her slogan under her senior class picture. I recently bought two hand-carved peace ring necklaces carved by an Onondaga woman, one for Chelsea to wear and the other for her sister, Mackenzie. In Native American thinking it serves as a reminder to stay calm and peaceful in times of stress. I also purchased "hearts of stone" for my wife and four daughters from this same woman. "A heart made of stone won't break."

CHAPTER THREE

PRE-COLONIAL TERRITORY

"The original country of the *Haudenosaunee* extended from the Hudson River to Lake Erie, from the St. Lawrence River to the valleys of the Delaware, the Susquehanna, and the Alleghany embracing the whole of Central, of Northern, and large parts of Southern and Western New York, as well as parts of other states. It was divided between the several nations by loosely defined boundary lines running north and south, which they called 'lines of property.'

Sid Hill tells me that there weren't established boundary lines so I'm sharing his knowledge with you on this topic. We whites have a tendency to have everything neat and orderly, defined, and accounted for.

The territory of Northern New York belonged principally to the Mohawk and the Oneida. The Onondaga owned a narrow strip along the eastern shore of Lake Ontario extending to the St. Lawrence River.

The line of property between the Mohawk and the Oneida began on the St. Lawrence River, at the present town of Waddington, and running south, nearly coincident with the line between Lewis and Herkimer counties, meeting the Mohawk River at Utica.

The country lying to the east of this line of property, embracing what is now the greater part of the wilderness, formed a part of *Ga-ne-a-ga-o-no-ga*—the land of the Mohawk. The territory lying westerly of this line, including the fertile valley of the Black River, and the highlands of the lesser wilderness, which lies between the upper valley of the Black River and Lake Ontario, belonged to *O-na-yote-ka-o-no-ga*, the country of the Oneida. The Oneida territory extended westerly to Deep Spring high on a hill outside of the village of Chittenango on Route 173. The north-south line ran through Deep Spring.

It was the custom of the Indians, whenever the hunting grounds of a nation bordered on a lake, to include the whole of it, if possible, so the line of property between the Oneida and the Onondaga bent westerly around the Oneida Lake, giving the whole of that to the Oneida, and deflected easterly again around Lake Ontario in favor of the Onondaga.

These three nations claimed the whole of the territory of Northern New York. But the northern part of the great wilderness was also claimed by the Adirondack, a Canadian nation of Algonquin lineage, and, being disputed territory, was the 'dark and bloody ground' of the old Indian traditions, as it afterward became in the French and English colonial history." (Sylvester pgs.14-15)

CHAPTER FOUR

EXPOSURE TO NON-AMERINDS

1492 AD Columbus reaches Watlings Island near Cuba, and Hispaniola in the Caribbean, believing he has reached India. The Scottish economist, Adam Smith wrote: "The discovery of America and that of a passage to the East Indies by the Cape of Good Hope are the two greatest and most important events recorded in the history of mankind." (Sale prologue) (My personal slant is that the Amerinds wouldn't agree. I'm sure they would rather have been left alone.)

1524 AD There was a major outbreak of smallpox in the Seneca Nation due to exposure to white traders from the southern regions of the continent (those that ventured up the western side of the Appalachians).

1534 AD As to Indians taken away into slavery, Cartier took 2 prisoners from the St. Lawrence River area in 1534; 10 were taken in 1536; 2 were taken captive in 1541. They died shortly thereafter due to disease for which they had no immunity. (Sale pgs.310-324)

1603 AD "Prior to European arrival, the inland lake areas of Champlain and Lake George had served for many years as an inter-tribal Indian warpath. The French arrived here in 1603, six years before the Dutch settled New York. Upon their arrival, they discovered the Adirondack tribe (called by the French, Algonkin [Algonuin]) to be at war with the Five Nations (called by the French, *Les Iroquois*)." (Bradfield pg. 8)

The Algonkin and the Iroquois were of two distinctive language groups. The Algonkin lived in Canada while the Iroquois were mostly south of the St. Lawrence River. The Algonkin were known as hunters and the Iroquois as farmers. This led to conflict in later years when wild game became scarce and the Algonkin could no longer trade venison for beans and corn. They invited the Iroquois to join their hunting parties only to find that the Iroquois were better hunters, as well. After feasting together one night, the Algonquin attacked, killed, butchered, cooked and ate their neighbors to the south.

In later years the French befriended the Algonquin, the Huron, and the Abenaki which they supplied with firearms. This put the Iroquois at a disadvantage until they could trade with the Dutch and then the British for weapons.

This hatred and jealousy of the Five Nations led the northern Canadian tribes, with the help of the French, to invade both the Amerind and white settlements of the Mohawk Valley. The village of Schenectady was raided one evening (Massacre of 1690) with the result that 60 white men, women, and children were massacred as they slept in their beds. Even the dogs and cattle were scalped as the houses were burned. This attack began a 70 [7] year conflict known as the French and Indian Wars [War]." (Bradfield pgs.9-12)

The Spanish, Dutch, French, and British were all exploring for territorial expansion and all had weapons in their possession to seize this new land. Native Americans could never have dreamed about such ships and firepower. Amerind survival depended upon the correct alliance.

> "The alliances established between the French and the Algonkin, and likewise between the English and the Iroquois Nation were almost inevitable. Differences in religious beliefs and opposing ways of life naturally divided the two European nations, and the deep-seated rivalries of the Indian tribes seemed to form a complementary interlace with those of the Europeans. Inter-tribal wars were intensified by the introduction of arms to the Indians

through trade…. In addition to firearms, the Indians now had need for other European items such as knives, axes, iron pots, and unfortunately, brandy and rum. By the time the first French settlers arrived in Acadia, the Indians of that region were already addicted to alcohol, and French brandy became the only article of trade with which the French could compete with the English and Dutch, who were able to sell most other wares cheaper.

…..The French came for furs and pelts and religious conversion. The English were not interested in building a new empire but escaping an oppressive one (I'm not so sure that statement is correct—it's quoted, but I question it). They established themselves as fishermen and viewed the Indians as merely a nuisance. The French relied heavily on transporting their goods (furs) from Lake Erie to Albany by way of the Mohawk River. New York fur traders, aligned with the Iroquois, saw this as an intrusion which was another factor leading to the French and Indian War." (Bradfield pgs.15-16)

1607 AD The French occupied Quebec (a few hundred settlers), and the English occupied Connecticut [eastern end]. (Sale pg. 388)

CHAPTER FIVE

ILLEGAL GAINS

1609 AD The States General of the United Provinces, known as the Netherlands (the *Vereenigde Oostindische*, called the VOC) was charged with the mission of exploring for a passage to the Indies and claiming any unchartered territories for the United Provinces.

(Here is an exact translation from the Dutch language to English in 1858 by John Romeyn Brodhead, Esq. as agent for Weed, Parsons, and Co., Printers.)

Holland Documents: IX

Brief and Clear Account of the Situation of New
Netherland; Who Have Been Its First Discoverers
and Possessors, Together With the Unseemly and
Hostile Usurpation Committed by the English
Neighbors on the Lands Lying There Within the
Limits of the Incorporated West India Company.

"New Netherland is situate [situated] on the north coast
of America, in latitude 38 to 41½ degrees, or thereabouts,
along the coast, being bounded on the Northeast by the
countries now called New England, and on the Southwest
by Virginia.

This district or country, which is right fruitful, good and salubrious, was first discovered and found in the year 1609, by the Netherlanders, as its name imports [imparts], at their own cost, by means of one Hendrick [Henry] Hudson, skipper and merchant, in the ship the *Halve Maene* [Half Moon] sailing in the service of the Incorporated East India Company; for the natives or Indians, on his first coming there, regarded the ship with mighty wonder and looked upon it as a sea monster, declaring that such a ship or people had never before been there.

The discovery of this country by Netherlanders is further confirmed by the fact that all the islands, bays, harbors, rivers, kills, and places, even a great way on either side of Cape Cod, called by our people New Holland, have Dutch names, which were given by Dutch navigators and traders.

In the year following this discovery, namely in 1610, some merchants again sent a ship thither from this country, and obtained afterwards from the High and Mighty Lords States-General a grant to resort and trade exclusively to these parts, as appears....in the year 1615, built on the North [Hudson] River, about the Island Manhattans, a redoubt or little fort, wherein was left a small garrison, some people usually remaining there to carry on trade with the Natives or Indians. This was continued and maintained until their High Mightinesses did, in the year 1622, include this country of New Netherland in the charter of the West India Company.

This Province of New Netherland was then immediately occupied and taken possession of by the said Company, according as circumstances permitted, as is the case in all new undertakings. For which purpose they caused to be built there, since the year 1623, four forts, to wit: two on the North [Hudson] River, namely Amsterdam and Orange; one on the South [Delaware]

River, called Nassaw {Nassau}, and the last on the Fresh [Connecticut], called the Hope. From the beginning, a garrison has been always stationed in all these forts.

The Company had erected these forts both Southward and Northward, not only with a view to close and appropriate the aforesaid rivers, but likewise as far as title by occupation tends, the lands around them and within their borders (being then about sixty leagues along the coast), and on the other side of the rivers, to possess, to declare as their own and to preserve against all foreign or domestic nations, who would endeavor to usurp the same, contrary to the Company's will and pleasure.

And for greater quiet and security, and, in order more lawfully to confirm their possession, the Company caused their servants to purchase from the nations there, as can be seen by divers [diverse] resolutions, deeds and conveyances, many and divers [diverse] lands situated in various places within their aforesaid limits, whereon boundary posts were erected, to which their High Mightinesses' arms were affixed, in order to notify other nations coming there that the country was owned and possessed." (Brodhead pgs. 133-134)

They go on to say that strong spirits, liquors, and distilled waters were brought in by arriving vessels to be sold by tapsters and taverns but seem to have been diverted to trading with the Indians. This brings on drunkenness whereupon they became rude, quarrelsome, and disorderly. It means taking possession of Indian land all the easier.

In all the documentation, I have not found any recorded deeds indicating purchase of land from the Amerinds by the Dutch. There is a great deal of communication about conveyance of property and deeds but no apparent evidence that they do, in fact, exist.

"Respecting the Dutch, the case is: In the troubles, when the Swedes came here, they were permitted to purchase in order to prevent the above mentioned lands being sold

15

by the Indians or natives to the Swedish nation. But your Honors will be better able to understand the whole matter by the grant and deed, whereof I shall endeavor to obtain copies, which I will transmit. Meanwhile I should not be surprised were men here to get some sort of lien on the above mentioned pretended proprietors; that is, to advance to them, if they should desire it, some money or merchandise, to wit, on a league of country or thereabouts, 50, 60 or 70 guilders at most, which, in Holland currency, is 50, 60 or 70 ells of Osnaburgh black linen; this is sold at 15, 16, 18, and even easily for 20 stivers (a stiver is worth 1/20 of a guilder), on account that they pledge their deeds and patents in return, by which means some title may be obtained, or any conveyance, mortgage or other incumbrance [encumbrances] thereon to the English may be prevented." (Brodhead pgs.52-53)

My own observation: Other than the acknowledged purchase of Manhattan for $24.00 (60 guilders worth of trade goods for 23 square miles of land), it seems that with the pressure on them by the British starting with the establishments of small British settlements on the Long Island, the Dutch are, as the expression goes, "between a rock and a hard place." The British are forcing their way on to property inhabited by the Netherlanders but not technically owned by them. They (the Dutch) occupy land on both sides of the North [Hudson] River some of which was illegally seized from the Mohawks. They had supposedly "purchased" two parcels, one being 2 leagues on the river and later a second parcel of 5 ½ leagues for which they were willing to pay 50 to 70 guilders per league. They are having great difficulty obtaining title or conveyance mortgage to show to the British that they did, in fact, pay for the property and are the rightful owners (there is no mention of the depth of the property, just the river frontage).

The British appeared to be the far stronger of the two nations trying to establish dominance in the area, i.e. more troops, more ships, and far more money. Once established on the eastern end of the Long Island, the British moved down both sides of the island in a westerly direction establishing small communities near coves and tributaries. They harvested and stole the crops that the Dutch had planted and quite often violent fights were the result. This pressure would assert itself for many years to come.

This land-grabbing arrogance by Europeans would then take a path up the Hudson to the Mohawk River, across Iroquois territory to the Miamis in Ohio.

May 20th, after the birth of Christ, 1653

"We declare that it is right and proper to defend ourselves and our rights, which belong to a free people, against the abuse of the above named government.

We have transported ourselves hither at our own cost, and many among us have *purchased* their lands from the Indians, *the right owners thereof.* But a great portion of the lands which we occupy, being, as yet, *unpaid for*, the Indians come daily and complain that they have been *deceived* by the Dutch Secretary, called Cornelius, whom they have characterized, even in the presence of Stuyvesant, as a *rogue, a knave and a liar*; asserting that he himself had put their names down in the book, and saying that this was *not a just and lawful payment, but a pretence and fraud….*" (Brodhead pg. 151) Italics are not original, but my emphasis. The Amerinds have already been waiting for 43+ years for payment that they'll probably never see.

The above doesn't surprise me when you consider the way that their Negro slaves were mistreated as documented in the volumes. They also brought children as young as 2 years old to this country to work for the almshouse [poorhouse]. Deceiving the Indians is just one more chapter in the name of Christianity. It gets worse.

"Previous to the American Revolution the seat of the Colonial Government was the city of New York, and the public records of the Province were kept there. They extended back to a very early period after the first settlement of the country. The most ancient of them were in the Dutch language; and they related to the affairs of New Netherland, as New York was called while it was a Colony and Province of the United Provinces, from soon after its discovery, in 1609, to its surrender to the English in 1664.

These Dutch records, however, are incomplete (how convenient for them). Missing are land transactions from Minuit (1626-1632), and Van Twiller (1633-1638). Those that were preserved are Kieft (1638-1647), and Stuyvesant (1647-1664)." (Brodhead Intro. vol. II)

CHAPTER SIX

TREATIES

* 1613 AD Probable date of the first treaty [alternate dates are 1677 and 1692] between the *Haudenosaunee* and the Dutch, signified by the Two Row Wampum, the *Guswhenta (Kaswehntha)*. For the *Haudenosaunee*, this formed the basis for all future relations with European settlers. It establishes the idea of two separate but equal nations that will respect one another's sovereignty.

"The Two Row Wampum Belt says: 'This symbolizes the agreement under which the Iroquois/*Haudenosaunee* welcomed the white peoples to their lands. 'We will not be like father and son, but like brothers. These two rows will symbolize vessels, traveling down the same river together. One will be for the Original People, their laws, their customs, and the other for the European people and their laws and customs. We will each travel the river together, but each in our own boat. And neither of us will try to steer the other's vessel.'

This agreement has been kept by the Iroquois/*Haudenosaunee* to this date." www.hometown.aol.com/miketben/miketben.htm

"The first treaty between the *Haudenosaunee* and the Europeans was recorded in the Two Row Wampum Belt in the early 1600s. Oral history has preserved the spirit and intent of that treaty as follows:

Before the Dutch people came to the lands of the *Haudenosaunee*, the *On-kwe-hon-weh* (The Real People)

lived very happily, enjoying life the way the Creator intended. The *Onkwehonweh* were dependant on nature, and taught the Dutch people their customs and artwork. The Dutch and the *Onkwehonweh* became friends so the Dutch said, 'We shall pronounce ourselves in friendship,' and they decided to make a Treaty and continue in friendship.

The *Onkwehonweh* called the Dutch, 'White People.' The *Onkwehonweh* held a special Council informing the people that the time had come for the White Race and the *Onkwehonweh* to continue as friends so that all the people might walk upon the Earth in peace, and love one another. When the *Onkwehonweh* and the White People understood this kind of friendship, it was made known by both races that the day had come to pronounce their friendship.

The *Onkwehonweh* said, 'We now have an understanding about our friendship so that the generations to come will also know about our friendship.' The Dutch replied, 'I will put our friendship in writing.' The *Onkwehonweh* replied, 'This is good, but we must never forget to pass it on to all the generations to come.' They agreed.

The Whiteman said, 'How is the *Onkwehonweh* going to describe our friendship?' The *Onkwehonweh* replied, 'We must thank the Creator for all his creations, and greet one another by holding hands to show the Covenant Chain that binds our friendship so that we may walk upon this Earth in peace, love, and friendship, and may we may smoke the Sacred Tobacco in a pipe which is the symbol of peace.'

The Whiteman said he would respect the *Onkwehonweh*'s belief and pronounce him as a son. The *Onkwehonweh* replied, 'I respect you, your belief, and what you say; but you pronounced yourself as my Father and with this I do not agree, because the Father can tell his Son what to do and also can punish him.' So the *Onkwehonweh* said, 'We will not be like Father and Son, but like brothers.'

The Whiteman said, 'The symbol of this covenant is a three link chain which binds this agreement made by us, and there is nothing that will come between us to break the links of this chain.' The *Onkwehonweh* said, 'This friendship shall be everlasting and the younger generation will know it and the rising faces from Mother Earth will benefit by our agreement.'

The Whiteman said, 'What symbols will you go by?' The *Onkwehonweh* replied, 'We will go by these symbols: When the Creator made Mother Earth, man was created to walk upon this Earth to enjoy all nature's fruits, saying no one shall claim Mother Earth except the rising faces which are yet to be born.

First, as long as the sun shines upon this Earth, that is how long our agreement will stand; Second, as long as the water still flows; and Third, as long as the grass grows green at a certain time of the year.

Now we have symbolized this agreement and it shall be binding forever as long as Mother Earth is still in motion. We have finished and we understand what we have confirmed and this is what our generation should know and learn not to forget.'

The Whiteman said, 'I confirm what you have said and this we shall always remember. We shall have respect for each other's way of belief, having our own rights and power.' The *Onkwehonweh* replied, 'We have a canoe and you have a vessel with sails and this is what we shall do:

I will put in my canoe my belief and laws; in your vessel you will put your belief and laws; all of my people in my canoe, your people in your vessel; we shall put these boats in the water they shall always be parallel. As long as there is Mother Earth, this will be everlasting.'

The Whiteman said, 'What will happen supposing your people will [would] like to go into my vessel?' The *Onkwehonweh* replied, 'If this happens, then they will have to be guided by my canoe. Now the Whiteman understands this agreement.'

The Whiteman said, 'What will happen if any of your people may someday want to have one foot in each of the boats that we placed parallel?' The *Onkwehonweh* replied, 'If this so happens that my people wish to have their feet in each of the two boats, there will be a high wind and the boats will separate and the person that has his feet in each of the boats shall fall between the boats; and there is no living soul who will be able to bring him back to the right way given by the Creator, but only one: the Creator himself.'

The *Onkwehonweh* called the wampum belt '*Gus-when-ta.*' The two paths signify the laws and beliefs of the Whiteman and the laws and beliefs of the *Onkwehonweh.* The white wampum background signifies purity, good minds and peace, and that the two peoples should not interfere with one another's ways.

The Whiteman said, 'I understand, I confirm what you have said, that this will be everlasting as long as there is Mother Earth. We have confirmed this and our generation to come shall never forget what we have agreed. Now it is understood that we shall never interfere with one another's beliefs or laws for generations to come.'

The *Onkwehonweh* said, 'What we agreed upon shall be renewed every so often so that the Covenant Chain made between us shall always be clean from dust and rust. We shall renew our agreements and polish the Covenant and when we get together to renew our agreements, we shall have interpreters; we will dress the same way as when we met so that our people will know who we are. I will put on my buckskin clothing, you will dress the same way that you dressed when you came to our people, the *Onkwehonweh.*' So they completed the Treaty of the Two Parties."

(Native American Center for the Living Arts-Winter 1980 edition-translated by Huron Miller <u>www.hometown.aol.com/miketben/</u> <u>miketben.htm</u>)

Each was acknowledging the sovereignty of the other. The treaty had to first be approved by the 50 chiefs of the Grand Council. The Council consisted of the Elder Brothers (Mohawk and Seneca), the Younger Brothers (Cayuga and Oneida), and the Fire keepers (the Onondaga). The Grand Council, I'm told, was presided over by the *Tadodaho*.

Prior to the treaty being finalized, the Two Row Wampum was placed in front of the other negotiating party. The two rows of purple beads are from the shells of the quahog clam while the white come from the Atlantic whelk shells. (*Akwesasne* Notes-G. Peter Jemison, Sovereignty and Treaty Rights 1995)

CHAPTER SEVEN

THE ONONDAGA-HURON (WENDAT) BATTLES

I n 1603 the French found the Iroquois at war with the Adirondack, then the most powerful nation in North America. When the French arrived in Canada, they quickly made friends with the Adirondack and a neighboring tribe, the Huron (Wendat). The Adirondack had previously forced the Iroquois out of their territory near Montreal. The Iroquois moved south and settled on the shores of some of the Great Lakes. They resolved that this treatment by the Adirondack would not happen again. They began preparations to better arm themselves.

Six years later in 1609, Champlain, who became the first Governor of Canada, joined the Adirondack in an expedition against the Five Nations. They encountered an Iroquois war party of some two hundred warriors. When the Iroquois heard the loud reports and saw the killing effectiveness of these new weapons, they retreated.

In September of 1615, Champlain again set out against the Iroquois but this time with the aid of more French soldiers and a war party of Huron. Moving down the St. Lawrence River (geographically down on a map, but up river in actuality as the St. Lawrence is one of a few rivers in the world that flows in a northerly direction), they arrived at Lake Ontario. Proceeding across the eastern end of Lake Ontario they came to the Oswego River. (There are differing opinions as to whether they then came across land to Oneida Lake and on to Onondaga Lake, or took a more direct route along the Oswego River which makes more sense to me as they would want to keep their canoes with them in case they were needed for a retreat.)

In any event, the Oswego River would bring them to "Three Rivers" where they could turn east on the Oneida River to Oneida Lake or maintain their course to the south on the Seneca River which would bring them to Onondaga Lake.

On October 9th they captured eleven Iroquois who were on their way to a fishing area. Champlain's account (N.Y.H.S. March 1849 translation) tells us that there were 3 men, 4 women, 3 boys, and a girl. (Clark pg. 253)

On the 10th of October, the war party arrived at the fort of the Onondaga. According to Champlain's accounts, the fort was built of four, large, interlaced palisades nearly thirty feet high. A fight quickly ensued and lasted about three hours until 500 Iroquois reinforcements showed up to bolster the fort.

During the battle, Champlain was severely wounded by arrows, once in the leg, the other in the knee. Unable to walk, Champlain was placed in a hastily constructed wicker basket, of sorts, and carried off in the retreat on October 16th. They placed their wounded in the center of the march while the front, rear, and sides were protected by selected warriors. The Huron chose not to return to Quebec by the St. Lawrence River route so they spent the winter with Champlain in Huron (Wendat) territory finally arriving in Quebec the following June.

The Onondaga fort on the shores of Onondaga Lake was later occupied by Sieur Dupuis in 1665, Count Frontenac in his expedition against the Onondagas in 1696, and by Col. Van Schaick in 1779 during the outbreak of the American Holocaust against the Iroquois. They reported that this particular area was lacking for trees and that it was a beautiful location. (The actual main village was located high on a hill several miles away, but since they didn't trust the French, it wasn't until 1655 that the location was revealed.)

It would have been nice if the ecology of the area were preserved, but by 1884 the Solvay brothers of Belgium had licensed William Cogswell and Roland Hazard of the U.S. to produce soda ash and thereby the polluting of Onondaga Lake, with extensive toxic waste material, started. Onondaga

Lake has the distinction today of being the world's most polluted lake. I'll discuss more on this later when we look at the Land Rights issues.

The Onondaga organized a retaliatory raid against the Huron near Quebec and when the Huron allies, the Utawawa and the Nipecerin, saw how fiercely the Onondagas fought, they left the area and fled west not to return again. The Huron, with some assistance from the French, were essentially "on their own" against the Five Nations.

1620 AD Estimated population of the various colonies: 2,498 I'm going to refer to population figures throughout the text to give you an idea of the geometric progression of increase in such a short period of time. This population explosion from immigration placed a great deal of pressure to expand westward creating multiple problems for the Native American inhabitants. The Iroquois were directly affected because of their geographic location. The Appalachian Mountains to the south, for the most part, were impassible forcing pioneers to a more northerly route through the Mohawk Valley and the very center of Iroquois territory.

CHAPTER EIGHT

DIFFERENT FAITHS

"[I]n or about the year 1625,] The People noticed that the European religion was spiritualistic in nature, the natural world being inhabited by numerous spirits both good (called angels) and bad (called demons). The People do not believe in demons but rather in mischievous spirits. The People only believe in one Great Spirit and do not see a need to worship him, after all, he is God and why would he need it.

The Black Robes, Society of Jesus, began their missionary activities in earnest among the 'savages' as they called them, and refused to accept that the barbarians already believed in the One Great God called the Spirit. The Spirit lived in all things not just man.

These French priests are not interested in the Peoples religious picture writings; their missions are to impose the French and European Christian beliefs and culture on a heathen and savage people, not to learn and adapt to a new land and culture.

These People held a strange belief that the meaning of existence is to maintain harmony with nature, a fundamental relationship with the universe. They talked of relations between man and earth, man and animal, man and God, good and bad, between sun, moon and earth, between sickness and health.

Free trade, free choice, individualism yet collective democracy, formed a Sovereignty Association. This type of discussion convinced the priests that such thoughts came right from the devil himself. It is noteworthy that most Europeans at this time believed King and Pope are infallible representatives of God and that any talk of freedom or democracy comes from the Devil as it challenges the Divine Authority of the leaders of civilization.

Native Beliefs:	*European Beliefs:*
Maternal stability	Paternal stability
Elevation of women	Women are evil incarnate
Freedom	Subjection to church and state
Democracy	Totalitarian
Tolerance	Absolutism
Sharing	Monopoly
Stewardship	Personal ownership
Mobility	Sedentary confinement to land
Good and bad	Universal guilt
Heaven for all people	Heaven only for Catholics/Christians
Natural sex	Self-denial
Pleasant after-life	Hell and damnation

There is no word for sin in the aboriginal languages. Evil deeds require compensation to the offended party. The taking of animals without first asking permission of the spirits is unthinkable.

Transgressions of this type are usually punished by the animal spirits that cause poor future hunts not as punishment by the Great Spirit. The Great Spirit is only offended if the People do not observe his teachings passed down through tribal tradition and ceremony. The Great Spirit doesn't issue laws to the People but rather suggests guidelines to follow in the People's quest for truth and understanding. The Great Spirit is considered a loving, patient, understanding God not one of anger, vengeance and intolerance as presented by the Black Robes.

The Jesuit's black and white view of the world restricts their ability to understand the People's culture. The Jesuits assumed the People were governed by chiefs like the Europeans were governed by kings and a Pope. They could not understand a society governed by a democratic process. The term 'chief' is not from The People but a European creation.

Asking for a tour of the Onondaga reservation in 2005, I was directed to make contact with Freida Jacques at the Onondaga Nation School. I went on a tour with several teachers that I figured were new to the district. Her talk often referred to the Good Mind and the Bad Mind as it applies to their beliefs of the Creation. I came across the following article written by her and revised on 9/19/00 which I want to insert here. Rather than me chancing an incorrect interpretation, these are her written words:

"Discipline of the Good Mind"
Freida Jacques—revised 9/19/00
Onondaga Nation

"Thousands of years ago, at a time when our people were in the midst of wars and pervasive violence, the Peacemaker came and brought us a message of love and peace. One of the gifts he brought to us at that time was the concept of the Good Mind (*Ganigonhi:yoh*). As children grow up in our Nation they hear the words 'use a good mind', many times. I felt that a deeper explanation of what using the Good Mind means would be beneficial and this is how I explain it.

When the Europeans first came to this continent they were surprised to see that the *Haudenosaunee* did not have a police force or many laws to encourage good behavior in the people. I feel that the use of *Ganigonhi:yoh* was so pervasive that it was unnecessary to have a police force and many laws.

I refer to the Good Mind as a discipline rather than just a description of a person's state of mind. First of all, *Ganigonhi:yoh* recognizes that we are connected to the good, that we have access to a loving source of good thoughts. Each and every one of us has many, many thoughts each day. With discipline we can become aware of each thought, see its substance, realize its intent, and then determine if you should follow and build on that thought. This realization that you have a will over your thinking is key [to this]. You have a choice to follow your thoughts based on a loving purpose (the Good Mind) or let go of thoughts and certainly not build upon thoughts steeped in anger and judgement [judgment].

In most cases it takes thousands of thoughts to get to a point where you are harboring hate for someone and capable of violence. This discipline helps us redirect our thinking to more constructive, kind and loving thoughts. Since our actions follow our thoughts, what we are doing with our lives will be kinder and gentler. Since the words we speak follow our thoughts, we also have a way of affecting the world around us with words that will reflect the Good Mind.

By observing our thoughts we may begin to identify areas in our lives that may need to be reflected upon and healed. Watch out for over-reactions to your experiences and also under-reactions for they may help identify places that need healing. Consider being more willing to look at these parts of yourself and seek out people who work as healers to help you work through old hurts and anger. Stifled anger never goes away; it lingers in the background ready to show up to add to your next angry moment. This can make for more dramatic moments than you want. Work through old anger and life will be less painful.

While we actively become aware of our thoughts, especially those that have a kind and loving intent; we naturally allow ourselves to become spiritually in tune with the Creator's wishes. This allows us to use our talents to fulfill our purpose on Earth. This is my motivation to follow the Good Mind, when it is time to leave this Earth I would like to feel that I fulfilled the purpose that the Creator sent me here to accomplish.

As *Haudenosaunee*, we give thanks to all the parts of Creation that make life possible here on Earth (the *Ganonhanion*). This keeps us connected with the very vital purpose of all living things. So our respect [and] love includes all parts of Creation. This understanding helps us use the Good Mind in our interactions with the natural world around us.

It has been said many times that change begins with the individual. If you want change to happen, begin by changing yourself. The discipline of the Good Mind is a process anyone can use to help him or herself change. Much can be accomplished with prayer, love and patience."

1626 AD Four Swannekens (Dutch traders) from Fort Orange (Albany, NY) joined a Mahican [Mohican] raiding party against the Iroquois Mohawk and are killed.

1628 AD The Mohawk are victorious in war against the Mahican [Mohican] and the Dutch. The Dutch and the Mahican [Mohican] were forced to abandon their settlements.

1629 AD The Black Robes (Jesuits) attempted to start schools for the children and introduced the practice of physical punishment that is foreign to the traditional method of child rearing. The Native mothers are horrified and refuse to send their sons to these schools.

1630 AD The Dutch arm the Iroquois this year so that they could put fear in their enemies (the French and English) and thereby secure more beavers for themselves.

1633 AD Three Jesuits attempt again unsuccessfully to reach the Huron (Wendat) country. The Jesuits are not liked by The People because they ridicule The People's behavior, [and] criticize their most cherished beliefs. They only tolerate their presence to preserve the alliance and trade.

1634 AD The Jesuits recommend creating residential schools for what they called the 'wild savage children' thereby giving the instructors the greatest freedom of discipline. The Jesuits feel that physical punishment is deemed necessary for education. The Jesuits believe that in order to convert the Iroquois, they must make them fear them."

www.agt/public/dgarneau/indian13.htm In 1637, two of the first six Native American children to enter the Jesuit schools end up being killed by beatings. That type of treatment of Native American children continued almost to present times.

1636 AD March 28th Twenty-three Huron are killed by the Iroquois and a request by the Huron-Algonquian council to go to war against the Iroquois is rejected.

May 13th The Iroquois attack a sleeping troop of Huron killing 12 without resistance. The balance fled.

September 2nd The Huron attacked 25-30 Iroquois who were fishing at the Lake of the Iroquois (Lake Ontario). They captured eight, killed one and spread the balance among the villages for a savage ritual of killing.

1637 AD The French marched against the Iroquois and lost the battle and the Iroquois retaliated by waging war on the French and their allies, the Huron (Wendat). The Huron built a fort at Three Rivers [Quebec] for fear of the 'Hiroquois', as they call them.

In April of 1637, a war party of Montmagny and Algonkin [Algonquin] attack the Iroquois but are defeated. Hostilities resume in June when a battle took place on the water between the Algonquin and the Iroquois. The Algonquin had smaller, lighter, and subsequently faster and more maneuverable canoes. The Algonquin were able to capture 13 Iroquois which they carried off in victory and later tortured.

In August of 1637 it is believed that the Jesuits brought disease with them to the various Native American villages. The Natives weren't ill until the Jesuits arrived. They looked at the religious practices of the Jesuits as practicing sorcery. The Jesuits reported that their unattended possessions disappeared so they shallow-buried contaminated blankets in the ground while being observed by the Natives. These blankets were infested with smallpox and influenza which they, the Jesuits, hoped would be discovered.

The Jesuits were given religious monopoly in New France provided that they also protect the fur trade monopoly. The Jesuits recorded it was a good day because so many 'savages' (People) had died. It was a grisly tally of saved souls [10,000] from their perspective. As these Natives were dying, they were baptized and upon death were considered martyrs by the Jesuits.

The Jesuits are warned that the remaining Natives plan to split Jesuit heads."

www.agt.net/public/dgareau/indian13htm pg. 5

1638 AD Swedish settlers [especially in Delaware] introduced the log cabin to the New World. Some Native Americans would adopt this type of dwelling in addition to the long house.

In 1639 the first recorded case of adultery between a White and a Native American accused Mary Mendame and an Indian by the name of Tinsin. Both were publicly whipped as punishment.

*1654 AD The French send Fr. Simon Lemoyne, SJ (Society of Jesus) to the Onondagas.

**Father Lemoyne, a Jesuit, is the first known white man to be in the territory of the Onondaga. It is claimed that he discovered the salt springs but I would guess that the Native Americans, having lived here for thousands of years, already knew about the springs long before his arrival. Historians are at odds about the reason for his settling in this area. One school of thought is his function as clergy in trying to convert the locals to Catholicism; the other is that he was a spy for the French or a combination thereof.

1655 AD There is an official monument dedicated to the fact that the very first Catholic mass in the Northeast (the very first was offered in St. Augustine, Florida by the Spanish) was celebrated on Sunday, November 14, 1655 by Joseph M. Chaumonot, SJ on the former land of the Onondaga Indian village situated on what is now called Indian Hill. Indian Hill Road is situated on a high bluff between Watervale Rd. and Oran-Delphi Rd. It overlooks the village of Manlius, New York and all points north as far as Lake Ontario. Brickyard Falls Rd., an old Indian trail, runs from Route 173, also an old trail, up to Indian Hill, if you're ever looking for a convenient route.

The high ground gave them a very strategic advantage in the early spotting of non-friendly, warring tribes (Huron to the north and Susquehanna to the south). They could see the campfires at a great distance and would be able to calculate how long it would take for the enemy to reach them and where specifically they were located by smoke from the fires. This fact was pointed out to me by an Onondaga at the Native American Festival held last year at Onondaga Community College (also situated on high ground). When not fishing near the rivers and lakes, camping on high ground kept them away from the *Anopheles* mosquitos and the many diseases they carried.

They had fresh, cold, clear water on both sides of the Indian Hill village. The east and west branches of Limestone Creek flowed by the village providing cooking and drinking water year-round as well as plentiful fish and mammals that fed on fish such as bear, otter, raccoon, etc.

"The village was elliptical in shape, about 1,050 feet long by 450 feet wide. There were about 140 houses (each house providing shelter to 4 families). The land was cleared and corn was planted there. The Indians raised enough so that they were able to trade with other tribes. It is probable that they also grew pumpkins, squash, and beans as we know that the Onondagas did use these foods.

About two miles south of the main village was a smaller one of about 24 houses. The village of the Onondaga was called *Onnontas*, or

Onnontague, from the word *Onnonta*, meaning 'mountain or hill.' These people were called *Onnontaeronnons*, or *mountain people* because they lived high in the hills."

"The Iroquois built villages that were surrounded by palisades. Palisades protected the people living in the village from attacks by other people. Palisades also protected the village from blowing snow in the winter and stopped wild animals from wandering in.

The Iroquois were agriculturalists. Corn or maize was the most important crop grown by the Iroquois. Corn was domesticated in Mexico and traded into southern Ontario by about 1000 AD.

Archeologists know they have found an Iroquois site when their surface collections of artifacts contain Iroquois ceramics and worked bone and stone artifacts. Clay pots and smoking pipes are decorated with designs used by Iroquois people. When archeologists find a piece of a pot called a sherd [shard] with these decorations, they can often tell which Iroquois group made it and how old it is.

The Iroquois people of New York built and lived in longhouses. Their houses are called longhouses because they were longer than they were wide. Longhouses have door openings at both ends. During the winter, these openings would have been covered with skins. There were no windows on the longhouse walls. We know this because the explorers and missionaries wrote that the insides of the houses were dark due to a lack of windows.

The longhouses were built by the men in the village. The wood for the houses was cut down in the spring when it was still flexible and brought to the village. The ends of the posts were sharpened into points using stone axes, and some were charred or burned to make it last longer in the ground. The walls of the longhouse were made from elm bark that was cut into rectangular slabs to be used for roof shingles and wall siding.

A post mould is the decayed remains of the posts placed into the ground hundreds of years ago by the Iroquois when they were building their longhouses. Large posts made of cedar were used to support the roofs of the houses and the benches along the sides of the houses. The posts look like dark round circles in the soil when they are found by the archeologist's trowel. In a cross-section, the post mould's straight sides and pointed end can still be seen many centimeters into the subsoil.

A hearth is the remains of a fire pit. You might have noticed that there are no chimneys in the drawings of the longhouses. Iroquois did not build stone fireplaces. Instead, they dug shallow pits down the center of the house. Above the fire pit there was a hole in the roof to let the smoke escape. The roof holes also acted like small skylights, letting a little bit of light into the dark, windowless longhouse.

Although the roof holes helped to let some smoke from the fires out of the longhouse, it did not let it all out. We know this because the missionaries and explorers complained of eye problems due to the amount of smoke inside the longhouses.

Hearths are identified by soil which has turned reddish by repeated use during the occupation....The area around the hearth is usually crowded with hundreds of tiny post moulds. These post moulds were made by posts used to hang meat near the fire for cooking, or to hang food or skins... for drying.

A storage pit is a hole that was dug inside the longhouse and used to store food. When a pit was used for storing food, we think that it was lined with bark and grass and covered with bark mats for lids. This was done to keep the food inside of the pit dry and to keep mice out....The pits could have been used for more than one year, but were abandoned once they were infected with mould or mildew."

www.rom.on.ca/schools/longhouse/longhouse1.php2/8/2008

"In the Iroquois community, women were the keepers of culture. They were responsible for defining the political, social, spiritual and economic norms of the tribe. Iroquois society was matrilineal, meaning descent was traced through the mother rather than through the father, as it was in colonial society. While Iroquois sachems (chiefs-leaders) were men, women nominated them for their leadership positions and made sure they fulfilled their responsibilities.

Besides performing the normal household functions of producing, preserving and preparing food and clothing for the family and taking care of the children, Iroquois women participated in many activities commonly reserved for men....they belonged to medicine societies (spiritual associations) and they participated in political ceremonies.

The Iroquois were an agricultural people and it was the women who owned the land and tended the crops. After marriage, an Iroquois man moved into the longhouse of his wife's family. Their children then became members of her clan.

www.iroquoisdemocracy.pdx.edu/html

The clan mother used to be the oldest but now is the most qualified (usually not a Christian because of the longhouse philosophy).

The Bear and Wolf clans originated near Oswego Falls, the Beaver and Snipe (Heron) on the shore of Lake Ontario, the Eel and Turtle on the Seneca River, and the Deer and Hawk in the Onondaga hills. (Beauchamp)

CHAPTER NINE

THE PIPE

"The Native American pipe ceremony is many things. It essentially opens the doors of perception by making the breath of the Great Spirit visual....It invokes the four quarters of the world: the East first, always the East first, the quarter from which the sun appears each day to relume [reluminate] the world; then the South, the land of fine horses, whence returns the summer and the grass and the world's fecundity; then the West, land of the thunder beings, which bring the life of the spirit and the storm clouds that nurture the winged ones, the two-leggeds, the four-leggeds, and the things that crawl the land; and finally the North, the source of the winter wind and the snow that scours the impurities off of creation; then the Earth itself, the kindly mother of all the fruits of existence; and finally the place of the Grandfather Spirits, the endless firmament of crackling blue sky." (Jenkinson pgs. 288-289)

**1658 AD Fearing for their lives, the Jesuits hastily left the small fort they built on the shore of Onondaga Lake. The story is told that wooden dug-out canoes had been built earlier and were hidden under a false floor in the chapel for such an occasion. This I learned from a tour-guide at the fort and not from a written source. This replicated fort (the French Fort) still stands on the shore of Onondaga Lake midway between Liverpool and Syracuse. There is an Iroquois museum, of sorts, in association with the fort manned by a volunteer staff.

**1661 AD For whatever reason, Father Lemoyne returns for a second visit.

1670 AD Estimated colonial population: 114,500 (a dramatic population increase in 50 years)

1680 AD Estimated colonial population: 155,600

"At its maximum in 1680, the [Iroquois] empire extended west from the north shore of Chesapeake Bay through Kentucky to the junction of the Ohio and Mississippi Rivers; then north following the Illinois River to the south end of Lake Michigan; east across all of lower Michigan, southern Ontario and adjacent parts of southwestern Quebec; and finally south through northern New England west of the Connecticut River through the Hudson and upper Delaware Valleys across Pennsylvania back to the Chesapeake. (Within this entire territory, only the Mingo occupied a small part of the upper Ohio Valley and the Caughnawaga in a small part of the upper St. Lawrence region.) www.jmu.edu/madison/center/main_pages/madison_archives/era/native/iroquois/bkgr...7/2/2007

**1696 AD Frontenac leads an invasion against the Onondagas (second village). They burn their own village which was situated on an old trail (present day Route 91 from Jamesville to Pompey) when they learn that his troops are advancing. They start preparations to move to their present village on Route 11 and 11A. This move was completed in 1720.

1711 AD Tuscarora War broke out in North Carolina

1720 AD Estimated colonial population: 474,388
Sir Robert Boyle established the first missionary Indian school.

*1722 AD Tuscarora are adopted into the *Haudenosaunee* Confederacy after being defeated in war by colonists in North Carolina who sought to make slaves of their people. They initially lived on Oneida Territory and in later years settled northeast of Buffalo, NY.
The Treaty of Albany created the Indian Confederation of the League of the Six Nations.

1730 AD Estimated colonial population: 654,950

1740 AD Estimated colonial population: 889,000

1744 AD Certain territories north of the Ohio River are ceded by the Iroquois League to the British in the Treaty of Lancaster signed at Lancaster, PA.

1750 AD Estimated colonial population: 1,207,000

**1751 AD Sir William Johnson [illegally] bought Onondaga Lake and shores.

"When European peoples invaded what is now the United States early in the seventeenth century, Native Americans responded with both interest and resistance. During the next three centuries, Indians and European Americans met, mingled, and fought a series of bloody conflicts. The Indian wars revealed much about the broader forces under-mining Native American independence. Although defeated militarily, Indian peoples emerged with their cultures intact. Survivors of the wars and their descendants today play vital roles in American life." (Violence pg. 80)

***1753 AD French troops from Canada march south; seize and fortify the Ohio Valley. Britain protests the invasion and claims Ohio for itself.

1754 AD May 28th, George Washington (not as a Patriot general) led troops in opening action of the French and Indian War.
*** Ensign de Jumonville and a third of his escort are killed by a British patrol led by George Washington. In retaliation, the French and the Indians defeat the British at Ft. Necessity. Washington surrenders after losing one-third of his force. "With Washington's defeat the French effectively control the Ohio Valley." (Bradfield pg. 17)

*** 1755 AD The British implement a plan to defeat the French. Major General Edward Braddock troops are defeated in the Battle of the Monongahela, and William Johnson's troops stop the French advance at Lake George.

*** 1757 AD The French led by Montcalm capture Ft. William Henry. Following the surrender, Montcalm's actions (releasing the prisoners to return to a different fort) anger his Indian allies who capture or kill hundreds of unarmed British on their retreat.

1758 AD July 8th, British and colonial troops are beaten by the French under General Montcalm at Fort Ticonderoga north of Albany, NY.

August 27th, the British capture Fort Frontenac.

August—the first Indian Reservation is established by the New Jersey Assembly.

*** William Pitt implements cooperative policies toward colonial legislatures to receive more colonial support for the war, the Treaty of Easton is signed with the Six Nations, and the British take control of the Forks of the Ohio.

1759 AD July 26th, the French abandoned Fort Ticonderoga.

September 18th, the French are defeated at the Battle of Quebec.

1760 AD September 8th, the French surrendered to General Amherst at Montreal.

1763 AD February 10th, the Treaty of Paris ended the French and Indian War.

*** Ottawa chief, Pontiac, unites many American Indian nations in an effort to drive the British off their land. Col. Henry Bouquet leads the British army and defeats Native American forces at Bushy Run.

King George III signs the Proclamation of 1763 reserving land west of the Allegheny Mountains for Indians.

*** 1764 AD The British Sugar Act is amended to tax the American colonies.

*** 1765 AD Sugar Act and Currency Act protests. Many colonies refuse to use imported English goods. Seeds of unrest are sown that will eventually lead to the American Revolution.

1768 AD Treaty of Fort Stanwix

1770 AD Estimated colonial population: 2,205,000

*1776 AD John Hancock, President of the Continental Congress, sends a wampum belt to the *Haudenosaunee* to show "good intentions" and "cultivate peace." (Yeah right!)

*1777 AD Background: Oneida and Tuscarora served alongside Patriot soldiers. Other *Haudenosaunee*, primarily Mohawk and Seneca, fought alongside the British, believing that they are maintaining treaty obligations with the British that dated back to the 1600s. For the most part, the Onondaga wanted to remain neutral. Free will is ever present, however, and some Onondagas had war-like tendencies and acted out on their own.

"The many are judged by the few."

CHAPTER TEN

THE AMERICAN HOLOCAUST

"Enjoy the war....the peace is going to be terrible"

During the French and Indian War, Washington was serving as a junior officer in the British Army and through his travels and surveying trips in New York and Ohio he could readily see that expansion would come through the present day Mohawk Valley. At 16 years of age he was an apprentice surveyor with Lord Fairfax. There were no direct routes through the Appalachian Mountains at the time. White settler/pioneer families with children and all their worldly possessions loaded on wagons could not make the trek over these mountains without established trails. However, by going around the Appalachian-Catskill range by way of the Hudson River Valley, this meant traveling on relatively flat land. Fresh water, fish, and game were available all the way to the Albany area. Here they could turn west along the Mohawk River bringing their journey to Central New York and on to the Ohio River Valley.

The major obstacles in this part of the country concerning travel were the local Amerinds and the *Anopheles* mosquitos. The Amerinds occupied the high ground while the mosquitos were prevalent in the swamps and bogs bordering the river. Many more would succumb to the bite of this female insect than by death from the war parties.

Washington could see that this fairly level route would be the path for expansion to the West. If he could secure land in New York and the Ohio Territory without having to watch over his shoulder for war-parties, there would be adequate land to sell to the migrating settlers, hence, a tidy profit in his pocket.

This led up to what became and is seldom explored, as the American Holocaust. Washington would later direct Col. "Goose" Van Schaik to march from Ft. Stanwix in the Mohawk Valley against the Onondaga Nation. The Onondaga at this particular time were trying very hard to remain neutral during the Revolutionary War. How quickly Washington forgot that the Iroquois, led by the Oneidas, fed his colonial troops and kept them from facing near starvation that previous winter of 1777-1778 at Valley Forge in Pennsylvania.

It is reported that troops under Van Schaik's command traveled the Mohawk River to Oneida Lake, where they crossed the lake to the Oneida River at the western end (Brewerton) then to Three Rivers where they turned south on the Seneca River to Onondaga Lake.

They camped on the shore of the lake where the outlet of the Onondaga River (Creek) meets the main body of water. Scouts for the Onondaga knew they were coming long before they arrived. In raiding the camps of the Onondaga, they mostly came upon women and children and the elderly (those that could not move rapidly). Although Amerinds attacked each other over the years, the elderly and children of other tribes were treated with respect and never bothered.

The captive children and elderly were promptly murdered while the young girls and women were taken back to the campsite. The Patriot soldiers aroused by their captives and their allotment of rum and in celebration of their victory over the helpless victims wasted no time in molesting and raping long into the night. I read where the first band of returning Onondaga, numbering maybe 29 members, tried in vain to pursue the murderers and rapists. They were vastly outnumbered as Van Schaik's troops numbered in the hundreds.

August 29th 1779, the American colonial army numbering 4,000 in strength also moved out of Pennsylvania north to Newtown in present day Elmira. Eventually facing them would be 600 British rangers and Iroquois warriors that were outnumbered 7 to 1. The Americans had ample food and ammunition; the Iroquois were starving and had used most of their ammunition hunting wild game for their families. Houses, towns, crops, clothing, orchards, and livestock, would all be devastated. (Mann pg. 86)

Geneva Convention on Genocide

Article II. "In the present Convention, genocide means any of the following acts committed with intent to destroy, in whole or in part, a national, ethnical, racial or religious group, as such:

(a) Killing members of the group;
(b) Causing serious bodily or mental harm to members of the group;
(c) Deliberately inflicting on members of the group conditions of life calculated to bring about its physical destruction in whole or in part;
(d) Imposing measures intended to prevent births within the group;
(e) Forcibly transferring children of the group to another group.

Unanimously ratified by the United Nations General Assembly on December 9, 1948

Begrudgingly ratified, in toothless form, by the U.S. Congress in February 1989

*Not in effect during the American Holocaust!

"Orders from George Washington— To THE BOARD OF WAR Head Quarters, White Plains, August 3, 1778

Gentlemen: I had the honor of receiving your favour [favor] of the 27th Ulto.[last month] on the 1st instant, inclosing [enclosing] sundry resolves of Congress and other papers respecting two expeditions meditated into the Indian Country one from the Southward and the other from the Northward. I have it [since the receipt of them], been endeavoring to collect the necessary information concerning the means already provided, or to be provided towards prosecuting the latter; and I sincerely wish our prospects were more agreeable to the views of Congress than they are; but after examining the matter in every point of light I am sorry to say, an enterprise of this nature at the present time under our present circumstances appears to me liable to obstacles not easily to be surmounted.

On receiving your letter I wrote to General Gates, copies of mine to him and of his answer to me are inclosed [enclosed]. I do not find that any preparations have been made for the intended expedition; If the project should be continued almost every thing is still to be done. The Board will perceive that General Gates imagined it was laid aside.

Governor Clinton happening to be in Camp, I took occasion to consult him and General Gates jointly on the affair. They both concurred fully in opinion, that a serious attempt to penetrate the Seneca settlements at this advanced season [and under present circumstances] appearances was by no means adviseable [advisable]; would be attended with many certain difficulties and inconveniences, and must be of precarious success. The reasons for this opinion are in my judgment conclusive.

Supposing the enemy's force is fifteen or sixteen hundred men according to the estimate made by the Board [and much larger by their accts.], (other accounts make it larger) to carry the war into the interior parts of their country, with that probability of succeeding, which would justify the undertaking, would require not less than three thousand men. And if the attempt is made it ought to be made with such a force as will in a manner insure the event; for a failure could not but have the most pernicious tendency. From inquiries I have made, not more than about twelve hundred militia from the frontier counties could be seasonably engaged for a sufficient length of time to answer the purpose of the expedition; little or no assistance can be looked for from the people of the Grants (Hampshire Grants are rangers from New

Hampshire territory-now Vermont), who are said to be under great alarm for their own security, which they think is every moment in danger of being disturbed by way of Coos (Continental Army ranger dragoons). The deficiency must be made up in Continental troops; and as there are only four or five hundred already in that quarter, who might be made use of on the occasion, the residue must go immediately from this army. The making so considerable a detachment at this time, is I conceive a measure that could not be hazarded, without doing essential injury to our affairs here.

Of this the Board will be fully sensible, when they are informed, that the enemy's strength at New York and its dependencies is at a moderate computation 14,000 men, our strength on the present ground less than [under] 13,000. Besides this number, only a bare sufficiency has been left in the Highlands to garrison the forts there. We have been lately reduced by a large detachment to Rhode Island, and it is possible a further detachment may become necessary. Should we weaken ourselves still more by an enterprise against the Indians, we leave ourselves in some degree at the mercy of the enemy, and should either choice or necessity induce them to move against us, the consequences may be disagreeable.

Though there is great reason to suppose the enemy may wish to withdraw their force from these states, if they can do it with safety; yet if they find their departure obstructed by a superior maritime force, it may become a matter of necessity to take the field, and endeavour [endeavor] at all hazards, to open a communication with the country in order to draw supplies from it and protract their ruin. This they will of course effect, if we have not an equal or superior army in the field to oppose them with. We should endeavour [endeavor] to keep ourselves so respectable as to be proof against contingencies.

The event of the Rhode Island expedition is still depending; if it should fail we shall probably lose a number of men in the attempt. To renew it, if practicable, we should be obliged to send reinforcements from this army, which could very ill be spared with its present strength; but would be impossible, if it were diminished by a detachment for the Indian expedition. And then should the enemy unite their force, they would possess so decisive a superiority as might involve us in very embarrassing circumstances. If on the contrary we succeed at Rhode Island a variety of probable cases may be supposed with reference to European affairs, which may make it extremely interesting to the common cause, that we should have it in our power to operate with vigor against the enemy in this quarter; to do which, if it can be done at all, will at least require our whole force.

These considerations sufficiently evince, that we cannot detach from this army the force requisite for the expedition proposed, without material detriment to our affairs here. And comparing the importance of the objects here with the importance of the objects of that expedition, it can hardly be thought eligible to pursue the latter at the expense of the former. The depredations [depredations] of the savages on our frontiers and the cruelties exercised on the defenceless [defenseless] inhabitants are certainly evils much to be deplored, and ought to be guarded against, as far as may be done consistent with proper attention to matters of higher moment; but they are evils of a partial nature which do not directly effect the general security, and consequently can only claim a secondary attention. It would be impolitic to weaken our operations here, or hazard the success to them to prevent temporary inconveniences elsewhere.

But there are other objections to the measure of almost equal weight. The season is too far advanced for the enterprise, to raise and collect the troops to lay up

47

competent magazines, and to make needful preparations and then to march to the Seneca settlements and back again would exhaust at least five months from this time; and the rivers would be impracticable before it could be effected. This time will not be thought too long, if it is considered, that the preparations of every kind are yet to be begun; and that when completed an extent of more than three hundred miles is to be traversed through a country wild and unexplored, the greater part hostile and full of natural impediments. The rivers too at this time of the year are more shallow [shallower] than at others, which would be an additional source of difficulty and delay.

I shall say little on the subject of provision, though it is a serious question whether our resources are so far equal to our demands, that we can well spare so extensive supplies, as this expedition will consume. Besides feeding our own troops, we shall probably soon have to victual the French fleet which is said to have twelve thousand men on board.

Notwithstanding the opinion I entertain of this matter, founded upon a knowledge of many circumstances which Congress could not be apprised of, in obedience to their orders, I shall without delay take measures for forming magazines at Albany [and upon the Mohawk River] and for preparing everything else for the expedition, except calling out the Militia and shall be glad of the further directions of Congress, as speedily as possible. If it is their pleasure that it should still go on, I shall apply for an aid of Militia and can soon march the detachment of troops which must be sent from this Army.

I shall take the liberty however to offer it as my opinion, that the plan for subduing the unfriendly Indians ought to be deferred till a moment of greater leisure. We have a prospect that the British army will ere long be necessitated either to abandon the possessions they now hold and quit these states, or perhaps to do something still more disgraceful. If either these should arrive, the most effectual way to chastise the Indians and disarm them for future mischief, will be to make an expedition into Canada. By penetrating as far as Montreal, they fall, of course, destitute of supplies for continuing their hostilities, and of support to stimulate their enmity.

This would strike at once at the root, the other would only lop off a few branches, which would soon spread out anew, nourished and sustained by the remaining trunk. Instead of the expedition resolved upon, it might be advisable to establish a well furnished garrison* of about three hundred Continental troops somewhere near the head of the Susquehannah [Susquehanna], at Unadilla, or in the vicinity of that place. And at the same time to establish a good post at Wyoming, with some small intermediate post. These posts would be a great security to the frontiers; and would not only serve, as barriers against the irruptions of the savages, but with the occasional aid of the Militia would be convenient for making little inroads upon their nearest settlements; and might facilitate a more serious enterprise, when it shall be judged expedient. I shall be glad of the sentiments of Congress on this proposition."

[Note: *The draft first estimated this garrison at 400 or 500.]
[Note: This letter is missing from the *Papers of the Continental Congress*]
(Washington, George, 1732-1799. The writings of George Washington from the original manuscript sources: Volume 12 Electronic Text Center, University of Virginia Library)

"The goals of Europeans and their descendants in North America led to portray Indians as enemies when the Indians were only defending their territories from conquest. The violence of the armed resistance by Indians allowed misrepresentations of the cause of that violence to be used by Europeans as war propaganda. The images of brutality (Wyoming Massacre) lasted as long as there were Indians defending their tribal territories.....Much remains controversial about the destruction of the indigenous people of the Americas, including the magnitude of the Indian Holocaust, its causes, and whether or not genocide is an accurate term to use in characterizing it.

There is no longer any question, however, that the near annihilation of the Western Hemisphere's native peoples during the four centuries following Christopher Columbus's voyages to the Caribbean constitutes the most massive human eradication in the history of the world.

Determining the size of the [Native American] population crash that followed in the wake of the European invasion of the Americas is an ongoing and difficult task. One of the more prominent, if conservative, estimates puts the proportional population decline throughout North and South America at roughly 90 percent, or close to 50 million people and perhaps as many as 60 million, between 1492 and the end of the nineteenth century. According to this conjecture, a decline of between three and four million people occurred in what is today the United States and Canada (Denevan 1992). It is not all attributed to wars and conflicts but the spread of diseases for which the natives had no defense took a large toll." (Violence pg. 76-77)

"With one extreme exception (Kroeber 1939), the *lowest* scholarly estimates made in the past of indigenous population decline in the Americas—estimates that are only one-third to one-quarter of today's conservative conventional wisdom—produce a hemispheric population collapse of approximately 65 percent. * This is identical to the proportion of European Jews who perished in the [European] Holocaust: for every three who were alive before the killing began, one was left standing when it stopped.

Using today's conventional estimates, the figures for the Americas are far worse: for every ten who were alive on the eve of the American Holocaust, one was left standing when the killing was over. And this is a conservative estimate; more likely, the extermination ratio endured by the native peoples of the Americas was twice this number. Thus in terms of both total numbers killed and proportion of population destroyed, there is no comparison: no event of mass killing in human history—the Crusades, the Black Death, the African slave trade, the Irish famine, the [European] Holocaust, the genocides in Cambodia or Rwanda—came close to destroying human life on a scale such as this." (Violence pg. 77-78)

What occurred on a regular basis during a treaty signing or a peace pipe circle were the gifts of blankets to the unsuspecting natives. These blankets were infested with diseases such as smallpox which rapidly spread through the tribes. These probably were some of the first documentations of germ warfare.

"When your army entered the country of the Six Nations, we called you Town Destroyer and to this day when that name is heard our women look behind them and turn pale. Our children cling close to the necks of their mothers." This quote is attributed to the great Seneca chief, Cornplanter, in a letter sent personally to George Washington in 1790 after the war. To Native Americans the words *president* and *town destroyer* are synonymous. Read on.

During the American Revolution, Patriot commander Colonel "Goose" Van Schaick and his soldiers attacked and burned Onondaga villages, killing at least 12 and taking 34 prisoners. However, nothing burned so deep in the Iroquois memory as the rapes and murders carried out by the Patriot soldiers at the Onondaga capital. An Onondaga chief recalled the incident: "When they came to the Onondaga town (of which I was one of the principal chiefs), they put to death all the [elderly] women and children, excepting some of the young women that they carried away for the use of their soldiers, and were put to death in a more shameful and scandalous manner; yet these rebels call themselves Christians." (Council at Niagara, December 11, 1782, in *The Haldimand Transcripts*, series B, The Public Archives of Canada, Ottawa, B.119, p.172).

In the meantime, Generals Sullivan, Clinton, and Brodhead invaded other *Haudenosaunee* lands to the west burning cornfields, food stores, and homes and killing the elderly that could not flee. Brodhead had pushed north from the Pittsburgh region toward Fort Niagara but his campaign stalled. Clinton and Sullivan met near Newtown, (present day Elmira)New York. Clinton arrived from Otsego Lake (present day Cooperstown) and Sullivan arrived from Pennsylvania.

Brodhead was to link-up with Sullivan and Clinton west of Canandaigua but this never happened due to Indian ingenuity (roadblocks and ambushes), and Sullivan's inefficiency. Sullivan's stalling tactics (he was never ready) caused delays in his troop movements.

The Indians have an expression: "The birds are out of their nests, but still on the wing." The Patriots may have chased them from their villages, but they were still a force to deal with. In past battles with other tribes, the warriors would seek the protection of the forest in advance of a war party. There was never a thought that the elders, women, and children would be mistreated—it was understood that they would be respected. Such was not the case with the Patriot troops.

The Patriot forces retreated after their assaults. The food that they had destroyed on their push to the north would have proved valuable to them on their retreat south. These actions against the natives encouraged many of the neutral Haudenosaunee to side with British forces in the War of Independence.

This should be covered in middle school and high school history classes as the Haudenosaunee Holocaust or, more frequently referred to as the American Holocaust but, God forbid, that something negative about George Washington should be written or discussed [a lie of omission]*. Just think, I portrayed him in a school play many, many years ago and was proud to be selected for the part. The innocence of youth! He chopped down more than a cherry tree!

* Lie of Omission: *"A lie of omission is to remain silent when ethical behavior calls for one to speak up. A lie of omission is a method of deception and duplicity that uses the technique of simply remaining silent when speaking the truth would significantly alter the person's capacity to make an informed decision."* (Choice 101 pg. 2)

Karl May, the German author, wrote about the American Holocaust and his writings were in Hitler's possession in his bunker at the time of his death. Hitler felt that the Americans would never enter the war on the side of the British and French. They had treated their own Holocaust issue with disregard and would probably ignore his land-grabbing and his mistreatment of the Catholics and Jews in Poland and elsewhere. From reading May, there are far more Germans that know the truth about the mistreatment of the *Haudenosaunee* than Americans acknowledge.

It must be shown that the concept of land ownership as "private property" was not known to the Native Americans.

"Indians fought among themselves over hunting rights to the territory but the Native American idea of 'right' to the land was very different from the legalistic and individual nature of European ownership. John Alexander Williams describes this in his book, *West Virginia: A History for Beginners*:

"The Indians had no concept of 'private property' as applied to the land. Only among the Delaware was it customary for families, during certain times of the year, to be assigned specific hunting territories. Apparently this was an unusual practice, not found among other Indians. Certainly, the idea of an individual having exclusive use of a particular piece of land was completely strange to Native Americans. The Indians practiced communal land ownership. That is, the entire community owned the land upon which it lived."

I just can't imagine that one day you have a home and the next day it doesn't exist anymore because someone took a torch to it. Your food and clothing are taken away. Your grandparents and younger siblings are murdered just for existing not to mention the unspeakable happenings to your mom and older sisters.

Native Americans now have a Holocaust Museum and web-site that they can turn to for correct information and for guidance in their lives. They can be reached by going to: www.nahm.org/AboutUs.html

**1781 AD Brant camped on Onondaga River (Creek).

*1783 AD U.S. War of Independence ends with victory over England

*1784 AD Treaty of Fort Stanwix cedes *Haudenosaunee* land north of the Ohio River to the U.S. (Onondaga territory is not affected.) During treaty negotiations, *Haudenosaunee* leaders were taken hostage (possibly in retaliation for siding with the British). In a meeting to discuss ratification of the treaty in 1786, the treaty was rejected by the Six Nations government, which quickly began appealing to the U.S. government for redress. This treaty followed an unsuccessful attempt by New York Governor George Clinton to negotiate land purchases from the *Haudenosaunee*.

**1786 AD Ephraim Webster, the first white settler in Onondaga valley arrived.

**1787 AD Benjamin Nukerk is the first white man buried in the Syracuse area.

*1788 AD New York State buys more than 96% of the Onondaga's land about 2 million acres from the Onondaga Nation. Onondaga territory is reduced to about 108 square miles but still includes a one-mile strip around Onondaga Lake. The purchase was made following a private effort to buy land and involved a treaty made with Onondagas who had no power to negotiate for their people. New York Governor George Clinton promised, "This tract is to remain with the Onondagoes (sic) forever. Our people will know that they cannot get any part of this tract and therefore will not attempt it."

(New York State had no authority to make treaties—only the Federal Government. Remember this point.)

**1788 AD Asa Danforth and Comfort Tyler arrive for the first time in the area. The area is first named Webster's Landing.

*1789 AD Treaty of Fort Harmar renews peace and friendship between U.S. and Six Nations. The Six Nations gives up claim to lands west of modern day Buffalo, but are guaranteed lands east and north of there.

*1790 AD The Trade and Intercourse Act requires Congress to authorize in advance any negotiations carried out by a state. The act states "that no sale of lands made by any Indians, or any nation or tribe of Indians within the United States, shall be valid to any person or persons, or to any state, whether having the right of pre-emption to such lands or not, unless the same shall be made and duly executed at some public treaty, held under the authority of the United States."

Estimated population: 3,929,625

**1791 AD Revolutionary War soldiers draw for lots on military tracts. (They are allowed to do this as the Federal Government is bankrupt and this is the only way that they can compensate officers by giving 600 acre plots of confiscated land. Some chose to sell this confiscated land to others and use the money for private use.)

A local historian, Kathy Crowell, submits the following remarks on Revolutionary War soldiers that settled in Central New York:

"John Cockley—was in the New York line, and served eight years, through the entire war. He was in both Colonel Van Schaick's and Colonel Nicholson's regiments. His property was ridiculously meager, valued at $2.37, and included a pair of spectacles, a tobacco box, and $2.00 in cash. He was 64 years old in 1820 and lived with his son Cornelius.

Samuel Clark—made his affidavit in May, 1827, when he was 71 years old. He had served about nine months under General Sullivan. Here is his description of his property: 'Real estate none, and never had any. Personal estate none, except my wearing apparel, consisting of one suit of home-made clothes, one spare shirt, and an old great coat.' He had no family.

Benjamin Darling—made three different affidavits in as man [many] years; all agreeing as to his service, but contradictory as to property. He was in Colonel Lamb's New York regiment nine months in 1782. He first testified that his property was worth $67.37, next that it was worth $270.37, while his debts amounted to $715.37. He owed Judge Miller $600, on which there was due $111 interest. In 1840 he was 78 years old and still a pensioner. He had two sons, Ezra and Alexander.

George Eager—made oath in September, 1820, that he was 74 years old, and had served as a surgeon in [the] New Hampshire troops during the war. He had considerable property, valued at $1,173, with debts of $500. He owned a part of lot 94 in Manlius, NY. In describing his household furniture, the old surgeon was facetious. He said he had 'one spare bed and bedding, one bedstead, crockery barely sufficient to make the family decently comfortable, ironware and other articles of household furniture barely sufficient to be comfortable, articles of provisions likewise' all worth $52. He then added that perhaps he might 'have an honest claim to two swine, nine geese, and perhaps six barnyard fowls' worth $11. He had living with him his son Samuel, a grandson, and his wife and her two children.

Hendrick Higbee—a Manlius blacksmith, served one year in the New Jersey troops, and had property worth $62.09. With him lived his wife and a grandson. The old patriot was 69 years old, lame and almost blind.

Joseph Hennigan—enlisted in Colonel Wynkoop's regiment, New York line, for one year, and afterwards re-enlisted for two years. He had $162.72 in property and owed $110.25 to William H. Sabin, Dr. Gordan Needham of Onondaga Valley, and Amasa Martin of Manlius.

Phineas Kellog—was 64 years old when he made his application, and had property worth $790.20, and debts of $365.13. He served one year in Colonel Jedediah Huntington's regiment, and lived with his wife and daughter.

Asa Merrill—was 85 years old in 1820, served in a Massachusetts regiment for three years, from May, 1777. [He] was a cooper by trade, and had six in his family, including his wife. His property was worth $378.95, while he owed $600.25. On account of his wealth his name was dropped from the roll, and in May, 1823, he made a second application, in which he demonstrated how his property had depreciated as follows: his set of cooper's tools were much worn and reduced in value; "1 saw," worth $1.75, was sold to Samuel Edwards in part payment for pasturing a cow; "grindstone," full half worn out; "fifteen barrels," disposed of to Messrs. Hull & Moseley for family supplies; "three old kegs," gone to decay; "staves, headings, etc., made up, help paid, and debts due Sylvanus Tousley, Reuben Bennett, Morris Hall (Hull) & Co., and W.& C. Gardner, paid;" "one barrel of soap," used up; "one axe, one wheelbarrow," nearly worn out, lent and lost; "two hogs, five pigs," fatted and eaten; "cash one dollar," expended in going to Onondaga to make the schedule in 1820; "debts due, supposed good and collectable," settled, except that of Slocum & Williams, and they dispute the demand; nothing received or can be from "debts bad;" one-half of pew in Christ Church, Manlius, disposed of to Sylvanus Tousley towards a note held against him for the pew itself. He was in debt at this time [for] $349.50. Merrill was still alive in 1840 at the age of eighty years.

George Ransier—applied for a pension January 25, 1825, when he was 69 years old. He had a long and varied military record beginning early in 1776, and was discharged in February, 1779. He immediately re-enlisted for nine months and served his time. In 1780 he served eight months as a bateauman, conveying provisions and supplies up the Mohawk to Fort Stanwix. He again enlisted early in 1781 for nine months, in Colonel Marinus Willett's regiment. His first application was not granted, for lack of proof, and in September, 1830, he again went before the court, when he said: 'I have never been in possession of money enough to go in search of evidence of my services in the Revolution, and even now have to rely upon the charity of my friends to get evidence.' He owned a quarter of an acre of land in Manlius [NY] worth three dollars, but not worth enclosing with a fence. He had bought a farm in 1807, of eighty-eight acres for $1,250; but in 1817 or 1818 he became involved in debt, and conveyed it to his son George for $25.00. He was living in 1840 at the age of 84, with his son George in Manlius.

**1792 AD Abraham VanVleck is the first white child born in Syracuse and Jeremiah Gould built the first frame house.

*1793 AD New York State buys 79 square miles (50,560 acres) of the Onondaga Territory. Onondagas believed that they were leasing land to New York State, not selling it. We, ourselves, are confused today by the language that lawyers use in their documentation of deeds, titles, and abstracts. Can you imagine trying to figure out what these documents meant without the mastery of the English language? We need a lawyer to be present at any real estate closing today to make sure of what we're signing. I'm sure it's not hard to pull a fast one on those that don't fully comprehend your language and are not properly represented.

** The first iron cauldron kettle used to boil salt arrives in the area. Asa Danforth builds his second mill in the area, a grist mill and saw mill on Onondaga Creek near the South Avenue Bridge.

*1794 AD Treaty of Canandaigua establishes peace between the U.S. and the *Haudenosaunee*, guarantees that the U.S. will not claim lands of the Oneida, Onondaga, and Cayuga Nations and accepts the right of the *Haudenosaunee* of "free use and enjoyment of their lands."

**Onondaga County is created. There is an Indian scare prompting the building of a block house at Salina.

*1795 AD The Onondaga sell rights to Onondaga Lake and the land surrounding it to New York State. The state is in clear violation of both the 1790 and 1793 Trade and Intercourse Acts. And like earlier treaties, these were negotiated with factions of the nation who had no authority to sell land.

*1799-1815 AD Handsome Lake appeals to *Haudenosaunee* people to return to the old values of kinship, family, and the ideas of the Peacemaker.

1800 AD Estimated colonial population: 5,308,483

1810 AD Estimated colonial population: 7,239,881

*1817 AD The Onondaga sell just over 4,000 acres to New York State.

*1822 AD New York State buys 800 acres at the south end of the Onondaga Nation, reducing Onondaga territory to its current size of 7,300 acres.

*1825 AD Erie Canal opens.

*1838 AD New York State attempts to have all remaining *Haudenosaunee* removed to a territory west of Missouri. This effort is thwarted.

*1847 AD The Grand Council Fire is returned to Onondaga Territory. The fire had been moved to Buffalo Creek by 1790 after being maintained at Onondaga for hundreds of years.

*1848 AD Syracuse becomes a city.

*1887 AD General Allotment Act, passed by the U.S. Congress, breaks up the communal land base of most reservation lands across the U.S. by subdividing the reservations into personally-owned tracts. But this act specifically exempts the *Haudenosaunee*.

*1924 AD American Indian Citizenship Act grants citizenship to Native Americans born in the U.S. The act contradicted the 1794 Treaty of Canandaigua and the 1815 Treaty of Ghent. Despite provisions of the law, certificates of citizenship were never distributed to any of the *Haudenosaunee*, so the law was never put into effect legally. Beginning with a letter to President Coolidge on December 30, 1924, the *Haudenosaunee* have consistently rejected U.S. citizenship. They want to stay separate as "the U.S. does not treaty with its own people."

1929 AD The Great Depression is not felt as strongly by the Native Americans. As Ada Jacques told me, **"they had little when it started, little while it was on, little when it ended."** Nothing changed, but they did have food and quite often shared with others. She told me of a white boy from a nearby farm she found sleeping on her porch who had no food. She brought him inside and provided him with a meal.

*1946 AD Following World War II, the Indian Claims Commission is established by Congress to redress past land frauds and treaties.

*Late 40s Some Onondaga land is taken as the result of a dam project.

*1947-1960 AD The New York State Power Authority confiscates 550 acres of Tuscarora land to build a hydroelectric dam and reservoir.

*1956-1963 AD Despite determined resistance by the Seneca; the Kinzua Dam is built, flooding 9,000 acres of the Alleghany Reservation, causing the relocation of 130 families and many graves.

*1970 AD New York State places a ban on eating fish from Onondaga Lake.

CHAPTER ELEVEN

WHOSE LAND IS IT?

* September 9, 1971 "Don't go near the road, the Troopers will get you." The Onondaga resist New York State's effort to take Onondaga Nation land to widen Route I-81. Negotiations in the longhouse lead to an agreement that prevents the expansion of Route 81 into extra lanes. An armed "braids and shades" conflict is avoided when the NY State Police are quickly called away to a different conflict—the Attica Prison Riot.

*1974 AD U.S. Supreme Court decides that the Oneida Nation's claim for lands which were lost through a violation of the Trade and Intercourse Act should be heard in Federal Court.

*1979 AD An agreement is signed between the Onondaga Nation and Onondaga County Sheriffs Department affirming that the Sheriffs Department will recognize Onondaga Sovereignty by not entering Nation territory without permission of the Chiefs except in life-threatening situations. This is not extended, however, to the New York State Police. There are rare incidents when the Syracuse Police enter Onondaga Nation Territory—usually in high speed pursuit from the city when they have called ahead to a chief for permission to enter sovereign territory.

*1980 AD Cayuga Nation files a claim for the return of 64,000 acres of land.

*1982 AD The Ancient Indian Land Claim Settlement Act seeks to resolve land claims by validating all prior land transfers and allowing Indian nations to sue only for monetary damages. The bill dies in Congress.

*1992 AD The Federal Government intervenes in the Cayuga case.

*1994 AD U.S. District Court Judge Neal McCurn rules that the Cayuga have a valid claim to their ancestral land.

*1998 AD Onondaga chiefs meet with Governor George Pataki in Albany to notify him that a land claim will be filed.

*2000-2001 AD After negotiations break down, the Cayuga claim becomes the first to go to trial in Federal Court. In February, a jury awarded the Cayuga $36.9 million dollars for their land and loss of use of that land. On October 2, 2001, Judge Neal McCurn announced his decision to add $211 million in interest to the jury award. An appeal of the decision is likely.

Timeline Credits:

* Robert W. Venables (NOON) Neighbors of the Onondaga Nation
** Franklin H. Chase Syracuse and its Environs Vol. I Lewis Historical Pub.
*** The War That Made America-French & Indian War Timeline-PBS 1/26/2006

CHAPTER TWELVE

THE STORY-ORIGIN OF THE FIVE NATIONS

D avid Cusick, an Amerind, was the first to write down the accounts of the Iroquois based on the stories told to him by the elders:

"The Holder of the Heavens instructed the people to advance along the bank of the river *Yenonanatche* (now the Mohawk River) toward the rising sun. They advanced eastward to the Great River, *Shaw-nay-taw-ty* (now the Hudson) where they camped for a few days. The people were in one language at that time.

Most returned the way they had come but some followed the Great River to the sea (Atlantic Ocean). They were instructed by the Holder of the Heavens to return westward.

The company advanced some distance up the river *Shaw-nay-taw-ty* to where *Yenonanatche* flowed out.

He altered the language of part of the group and named them *Te-haw-re-ho-geh* (now the Mohawk). Their territory would follow the banks of the *Yenonanatche* for a two and one-half day walk until they came to a creek called *Kaw-na-taw-te-ruh* (near the Susquehanna). This group's language was also altered from the main group and they were named *Ne-haw-re-tah-go* (Oneida).

The main group proceeded toward the setting sun still under the direction of the Holder of the Heavens. The third family was directed to make their residence on a mountain and they were given the name *Seuh-now-kah-tah* (Onondaga). Their language was also altered as the Mohawk and Oneida.

The remaining company continued their journey towards the sunsetting (his words). The fourth family was directed to make their residence near a long lake named *Go-yo-goh* and the family was named *Sho-nea-na-we-to-wah* (Cayuga) and their language was altered as well.

The fifth family was directed to make their residence south of *Jenneatowake* (Canandaigua Lake) and the family was named *Te-how-nea-nyo-hent* (Seneca). Their territory was approx. between the Genesee River and the Niagara River.

The Holder of the Heavens forms the mode of Confederacy which was named *Ggo-nea-seab-neh* (Long House). An agent from the superior power visits the families and instructs them in various things respecting matrimony, moral rules, and worship. He warns them an evil spirit is in the world and will induce them to commit trespasses against the rules. Obedience to rules would give them a place of happiness; disobedience results in a state of misery.

He gives them the seeds of corn, beans, squash, potatoes, and tobacco with directions on how to cultivate them. He instructs them about taking care of the wild game and their territory in general (ecology). He departs and does not return.

The Long House became numerous and powerful; the Mohawk had 5,000 warriors; the Oneida had 3,500 warriors; the Onondaga had 4,000 warriors; the Cayuga 4,500 warriors; and the Seneca had the most with 6,000 warriors. In 1650, Cusick gives us an estimated strength of Iroquois warriors at 25,000. In 1677, Greenhalgh estimates their strength at 10,000 warriors. Continual wars destroyed their warriors rapidly, but these were partially replaced by the adoption of captives.

The Mohawk were to watch for enemies to the rising sun, the Seneca were appointed to watch the west where the sun sets. The Onondaga were the keeper of the Council fire. These were the prominent tribes. The sister tribes were the Oneida and the Cayuga later to be joined by the Tuscarora.

The Tuscarora, about 150 years before the arrival of Columbus, sent messengers to have talks with the five nations. They had twenty-four large towns and could muster some 6,000 warriors. Their territory, at the time, was between the seashore and the mountains which divide the Atlantic states (that's as specific as he gets). Hostilities between the Tuscarora and their southern neighbors broke out into a war that lasted, Cusick says, for several years. They asked for aid from their five nation friends and with their help, ended hostilities.

As a result of the war, the laws of the Confederation provide that the Onondaga will furnish a King and the Mohawk will provide a War Chief for the nations." (Cusick pgs.11-36)

++ This part is particularly interesting since it was dreamed 150 years before the arrival of Christopher Columbus, and The People had never heard of nor seen whites.

King *Atotarho* XI, of the Onondaga, in a dream, "foretells that the whites would cross the Big Waters and bring liquors with them, and buy up the red people's land; he advises them not to comply with the wishes of the whites, lest they should ruin themselves and displease their Maker; they would destroy the tree of peace and extinguish the Great Council Fire at Onondaga, which was so long preserved to promote their national sovereignty." (Cusick pg. 37)

At this time, the Mohawk were at war with the Mohegan on the other side of the Hudson. They asked for assistance from their brothers, the Oneida and Onondaga which tribes also crossed the river in such force that the Mohegan sued for peace. War also broke out on the western border with the Erie warriors. With the alliance of the five nations, the Erie were forced out of *Haudenosaunee* land and were incorporated with southern tribes. The kingdom enjoyed many years of peace after these wars. (Cusick pg. 38)

Cusick was the son of a Tuscarora who lived on a reservation near Lewiston, NY. The father, Nicholas Cusick, died at age 82 in 1840. David, who contributed much to this writing, died soon after his father. The Tuscarora, at the time, had villages among the Oneida. David had a brother, James who later became a Baptist minister.

CHAPTER THIRTEEN

RELIGION

Tuscarora Village, June 10th, 1825
David Cusick writes of the foundation
of the Great Island

A mong the ancients there were two worlds in existence. The lower world was in great darkness possessed by a great monster; but the upper world was inhabited by mankind. There was a woman who conceived twins. While she was weary she fell asleep and started to descend toward the dark world. Coming out of the sky, she was descending down to the great water.

A large turtle came forward and proposed that he could support her weight so she wouldn't sink further into the water. While holding her, the turtle increased in size every moment and became a considerable island of earth, and became covered with bushes.

The woman, during her delivery, was in considerable pain and died shortly after delivering twins. The twins inhabited the Dark World while the turtle island increased in size. When the infants were grown up, one of them possessed a gentle disposition and was named *Enigorio*, i.e., the Good Mind. The other youth had an insolent character, and was named *Enigonhahetgea*, i.e., the Bad Mind. The Good Mind was not content to remain in the Dark World but the Bad Mind was desirous to remain.

The Good Mind decides to create a better world than to live in darkness. He took the deceased parent's head and created a great orb of light to brighten the new world. This orb became the sun which would give light to the day. The rest of the body became another orb (the moon) which was inferior to the sun but would give light to the night. The Good Mind then proceeded to create spots of light (stars) which would regulate the days, nights, seasons, years, etc.

The Good Mind continued the works of creation, and he formed numerous creeks and rivers on the Great Island, and then created numerous species of animals of the smallest and greatest, to inhabit the forests, and fish of all kind to inhabit the waters.

When he had made the universe, he was in doubt respecting some being to possess the Great Island. He formed two images of the dust of the ground in his own likeness, male and female. He breathed into their nostrils and gave them life and named them *Ea-gwe-howe*, i.e., Real People. He gave the people all the animals of game for their nourishment, thunder to water the earth by frequent rains, and vegetation for the animals.

At the same time, the Bad Mind was creating high mountains and water-falls and he created reptiles that would be harmful to the Real People. The Bad Mind also created images but of clay which took the form of apes.

A two day fight ensues as to who will have control over the people while alive on the turtle's back. The Good Mind is victorious and it is decided that the Bad Mind will have power over the souls of mankind after death. He sinks down to eternal doom and becomes the Evil Spirit.

An alternate story that I read at the Iroquois Museum near Cobleskill, NY was that Sky-woman gave birth to Mother Earth and that Mother Earth gave birth to the Good Mind and the Bad Mind. The Navajo will tell you that they came out of the ground, not the sky.

CHAPTER FOURTEEN

LACROSSE

Sacred Sport

"**B**arry Powless once did the unthinkable. He left his lacrosse stick in the rain. Powless, a Native American, woke up the next morning to his father's reprimand, 'Where is your lacrosse stick?' His eyes got wide. His heart sank. He had committed something akin to a sin among Native Americans.

The shame of the deed weighed heavily on Powless' mind. Lacrosse, he learned, is a sacred activity among the Iroquois. It can act as a substitute for war, as a medicinal ceremony, as a unifier of the six Iroquois nations. Its equiptment [equipment] is so revered that the Iroquois are often buried with their lacrosse sticks, made of hickory and cow gut, hand-carved and cured for as long as a year.

For Powless at the time, it was pretty heavy stuff. 'It was then that I realized just what the stick ment [meant],' Powless said. 'I came away with a better understanding of what the game meant to my people.'

'It was like him leaving his arm out there,' said Wes Patterson, a Native American and master stick carver. 'Your stick is part of you. It is a sacred thing. Leaving it out in the rain…it's like cutting your arm off and throwing it in the lake.'

Lacrosse has been integral to the Iroquois culture for more than a thousand years. Families were known for their prowess in the sport.

Children were given a stick as soon as they could walk. It was, and still is, much more than a game." (Marcus Hayes)

If my memory serves me well, when I was a youngster, the only lacrosse teams that I heard about were two local high schools those being West Genesee and Lafayette. There was a third, Irondequoit, but that was far away in the Rochester area. Compared to those days the sport has increased dramatically in popularity.

I had no idea what the game was all about, so when I found out that Syracuse University was playing a lacrosse game on a particular Saturday, it sparked my curiosity. My mom told me that the field was not all that far from our house and that I could get there easily on my bike.

The interest in the game back then was nothing compared to the audience of today. When I arrived, there were maybe 60 to 70 people on both sides of the field—that was it! It was raining and we all stood in mud—no bleachers back then. There were several huge men running around and passing a small, white, rubber ball to each other from nets attached to sticks. The men wore shorts and a sport jersey but no padding except for the goalie.

One large, black individual that I remember in particular, would carry the ball in his net and it seemed that others, in different colored uniforms, tried in vain to get it away from him. They were literally bouncing off this guy who I later learned was Jim Brown. He was not only a stand-out in lacrosse but lettered in track and went on to the pros in football. He was an All-American in lacrosse while at Syracuse.

There were many stand-outs at Syracuse from the reservation and after doing some research I've come up with these names out of many:

Freshman scoring records:

8th Oliver Hill 50 points—37 goals, 13 assists (1972)
9th Barry Powless 42 points—22 goals, 20 assists (1976)
14th Sid Hill 34 points—11 goals, 23 assists (1971)

Single season saves:

5th Travis Solomon 54 (1983)

Most goals in a single season:

21st Verne Doctor 42 (1968)

Career goals:

25th Verne Doctor 90 (1971-72, 1974)

Most goals in a single game:

Greg Tarbell tied with Casey Powell and Gary Gait for most goals scored in a game, 9 in 1982 against Bucknell U. Tarbell was previously on the 1978 Boy's High School All-American Team on attack for Lafayette High School. I remember him throwing the ball harder and faster than anyone else I've ever seen. He was the impetus for change in netting composition. More shots of his would tear through cotton netting causing the game to be stopped while it was repaired. It wasn't long after that poly material became prevalent.

Ron Hill, 7 in 1972 against Clarkson
Oliver Hill, 7 in 1972 against Union
Ron Hill, 7 in 1971 against Colgate

There are others like Freeman Bucktooth and his son Brett that both played at S.U. not to mention others like Ron Doctor, David Waterman, Emmett Printup, Marshall Abrams, Solomon Bliss, and AJ Bucktooth. I believe Gewas Schindler played for Loyola. One to enter the National Lacrosse Hall of Fame was Oren Lyons, Jr. He was a 3rd team All American in 1957 and 1958 and an Honorable Mention in 1956 at Syracuse. Along with his lacrosse accolades he is Faith Keeper of the turtle clan of the Iroquois Confederacy.

I mentioned how few were at the first outdoor game I attended but I want you to know that 18,458 were in attendance in 1990 when Syracuse played Hobart at the Dome. The overall record for an indoor game was an NCAA game when Syracuse played Cornell—20,007.

The Onondaga play both forms of lacrosse. They play the field game while attending high school at La Fayette and also the box lacrosse version at their own indoor arena, called *Tsha'Hon'nonyen'dakwa'* on Route 11 which passes through the reservation.

Besides the Native Americans that achieved success at Syracuse University, the accomplishments of the following while at Onondaga Community College (OCC) needs mentioning here. These young men contributed greatly in helping OCC win the NJCAA National Championship in 2006 and 2007:

ROSTERS

2006: Kevin Bucktooth, Jr.—Syracuse U. (Lafayette H.S.)
   Sid Smith—Syracuse U.   (Six Nations-Canada)
   Matt Myke   (Six Nations-Canada)
   Craig Point   (Six Nations-Canada)
   Lee Nanticoke—Syracuse U. (Lafayette H.S.)
   Kent Squires-Hill—Syracuse U. (Six Nations-Canada)*
   Cody Jamieson—Syracuse U. (Six Nations-Canada)
   Ross Bucktooth—Limestone (Lafayette H.S.)

2007: Cody Jamieson—Syracuse U. (Six Nations-Canada)
   Isaiah Kicknosway—
   Minnesota Swarm (pro) (Walpole Island-Canada)
   Ross Bucktooth—Limestone (Lafayette H.S.)
   Tyler Hill—Hobart   (Lafayette H.S.)
   Jeremy Thompson—Syracuse U. (Lafayette H.S.)
   Jerome Thompson—Syracuse U. (Lafayette H.S.)
   Holdon Vyse   (Six Nations-Canada)
   Lee Nanticoke—Syracuse U. (Lafayette H.S.)
   Kent Squires-Hill—Syracuse U. (Six Nations-Canada)*
   Logan Kane   (Kahnawake-Canada)
   Lee Thomas   (Akwesasne-Canada)
   Wade Bucktooth   (Lafayette H.S.)

* Kent Owen Hill (a.k.a. Kent Squire Hill) was charged with second degree murder in Brantford, Canada in the death of his ex-girlfriend, Tashina General. Kent Hill supposedly was recruited by Syracuse University.

2008:	Holdon Vyse	(Six Nations-Canada)
	Cody Johnson	(Six Nations-Canada)
	Logan Kane	(Kahnawake-Canada)
	Lee Thomas	(Akwesasne-Canada)
	Wade Bucktooth	Lafayette H.S.
	Ely Longboat	(Six Nations-Canada)
	Coady Adamson	(St. Stephen's-Canada)
	Mike Buck	(St. Catherine's-Canada)

These stats are courtesy of Chuck Wilbur who is the Recruiting Specialist and Head Coach at Onondaga Community College. O.C.C. was the National Champion in their division NJCAA in 2006 and 2007. If you are interested in the program at O.C.C. he can be contacted at Wilburc@sunyocc.edu or (315) 498-2164.

I have come up with a short list of Native American players that went into the pros. If you know of others, please let me know.

Gewas Schindler—New York, Colorado, Arizona,
Columbus, and Philadelphia
Regy Thorpe—Rochester
Brett Bucktooth—Buffalo
Travis Hill—Minnesota
Barry Powless—Buffalo
Delby Powless—Buffalo
Neal Powless—Buffalo, New Jersey, Columbus, Syracuse,
and Rochester
Marshall Abrams—Rochester, Columbus

On Saturday April 15, 2006 there was an historic game played at the Onondaga Nation Arena that I was able to witness. It was an all Native American team (Onondaga) versus an all African-American team from

Howard University. The Onondaga Redhawks had 20 players that day while the Howard "Storm" could only muster 10. The Howard University coach, Duane Milton, presented some African artifacts as gifts and Alf Jacques, the assistant head coach and general manager, presented an inscribed lacrosse stick that he made to commemorate the historic game.

Howard's Kareem McKnight had this to say, "I really enjoyed playing the game and had fun out here. It's not about win or lose. It's about coming out here, having fun and bringing the black youth and the black players up to the level where we should be playing with everybody else."

Neal Powless who starred at Lafayette High School, Nazareth College, and a pro team, the San Francisco Dragons, wanted to be a part of history playing against an all African-American team.

Though it was a fun-filled afternoon for both teams, it would be an even longer bus ride home for the Howard "Storm" as they were out-played 15-0.

I haven't meant to leave the girls out but in case you weren't aware, Native American girls don't play the game unless they have left the reservation. It is strictly considered a man's game so much so that they are discouraged from even picking up a stick. Over the past few years I have known but three girls that played for Fayetteville-Manlius H.S. that were non-residents of reservations. One was Oneida, one was Mohawk, and the third was Cherokee.

For me, I witnessed history again on Sunday the 24th of February, 2008. I saw another college girl's lacrosse game at the Dome. It wasn't the game that was unique, but who was playing. On attack against Dartmouth, and scoring 4 goals for Syracuse, was a young Native American gal by the name of Awehiyo Thomas from the Six Nations Territory in Canada. According to the S.U. program she is a transfer student. I know of another gal who has ties to the Onondaga but I'll let that story develop on its own. I wouldn't want to steal the thunder from her very proud father. I saw her play in high school and I know that she can hold her own at whatever college she chooses—though I'm partial to seeing her play in the future at Syracuse University!

The prime sport for the girls on the reservation seems to be softball besides their intramural sport participation in school.

CHAPTER FIFTEEN

DANCES

The dances that I have observed over the past few years have been all "social" dances. These are performed in public and quite often outsiders are invited to join in and participate. Most are danced just for the joy of it. They might include such dances as the robin dance, duck dance, the alligator, friendship dance, traditional, ladies traditional, grass dance, fancy shawl, fancy dance, fishing dance, and my favorite—the smoke dance.

The dances for the most part are not taught, they are learned from observation. Children watch their parents or older siblings from an early age. They can enter dance competitions at many pow-wow locations around the country; and by observing their competitors they can sense what the judges are looking for as they perfect their own technique and style.

Tribal dances from other areas might include hoop dances, fancy dances, jingle dances, or chicken dances among others which reflect particular dance steps and clothing of other regions of the country. I enjoy the variety that a major pow-wow presents. A few years ago I had the opportunity to spend three fun-filled days off Route 2 in Mashantucket, Connecticut at the *Schemitzun* held at Fox Run Casino.

The pow-wow/festival is held every August and if you share the same interest and enthusiasm that I do, I would highly recommend it. There are approximately 2,000 dancers and 65 drum bands from all over Mexico, Canada, and the U.S. The Grand Entry of dancers takes more than an hour to complete. It is held in a tent that is probably the size of two football fields end-to-end and 100 yards wide. It is known as the World Championship of Native American song and dance.

The "*pow-wass*" to the Native Americans is "the gathering of people." The "pow-wow" is the white version. It is open to the public and if you stay on Mashantucket-Pequot property, there is shuttle service to the *Schemitzun* grounds. There are vendor tents set up around the perimeter for Native American clothing, jewelry, music, carvings, books, and food. You can experience the cuisine of buffalo, elk, venison, fry bread, corn soup, strawberry drink, and chili tacos. I was very impressed by the buffalo brisquet.

Don't expect to get a beer with your sandwich as the grounds are drug and alcohol free and it's strictly enforced. You can bring a camera but in most cases they suggest that you ask first before taking someone's picture. Some Amerinds feel like the Chinese do—that you are removing a part of their spirit.

I'm not mentioning all the dances here just the social ones as the ceremonial dances are closed to non-Native Americans as are some festivals; hence, no information as it is private.

Michael Thomas (a Pequot councilor) writes: "To us it is a celebration that we're still here. It is an opportunity to again, as we once did very often, share intertribal culture with other tribes and scream from the highest mountaintop that we've never gone anywhere."

Boye Ladd (Ho Chunk Nation): "We look to *Schemitzun* as perhaps being our national finals, our biggest championship for the year...."

Johnny Whitecloud (Otoe-Creek): "The culture, the tradition, the spirituality, the language preservation, the song and dance-it's meaningful to all of us. *Maz-ayre-os say juan-guz-a-duh*—it means to be searching, grasping in the dark for something to latch onto. So this is how we hang onto our, all of our culture, spirituality and our traditions and still yet coexist, peacefully coexist in a dominant society.....So we have forgiveness and then we pray for the people that oppressed us and there the Creator's watching us and then he's going to bless our children accordingly. We forgive so that we can carry on and have our children grow up in a real good way and still hang onto their identity living in this dominant society."

Marvin Burnette (Rosebud Sioux Lakota): "And we as Native people, whenever we go to a pow-wow, usually our third song is always a veteran's honoring song. As warriors, we wear the eagle feather, we as veterans we respect the American flag, the red, white and blue. And every one of our events includes the American flag, although I cannot forget that the first flag was the Indian flag, a single eagle feather on a wooden staff."

April Whittemore (Lumbee-Cheraw, Irish): "I love pow-wows. I love to pow-wow. Pow-wows have helped me as a young person. When I was in junior high I had low self esteem because of the identity. I associated myself with a Hispanic because outside that's how I looked even though I knew I was Native American I said, well, I'm gonna hang with this group because this is what I look like. Okay, and I got into pow-wows, I learned about the elders, the veterans, the dancing, why you dance. Dancing's the least of the pow-wow, it's why you do it, why do you wear these colors, what has your grandmother or your grandfather taught you? So all of that just brought my self-esteem up. I said, I know who I am and I'm Indian and I'm proud, I'm Irish and I'm proud. So when I understood those things and my self-esteem just rose, my grades rose, and I had a direction in my life, so that helped me a lot." [The grammar is hers.]

Terry Fiddler (Cheyenne River Sioux): "Our main goal as tribal people is to protect our sovereignty, our jurisdiction of our reservation and our way of life. For many years the government had banned our religious ceremonies, even our dancing. People had to sneak off and do the ceremonies and dances in secret. And I guess that's what laid upon each generation that comes is to protect what we have left and see that it's passed onto the next generations. My grandparents are the ones that taught me the dancing and singing. We used to pow-wow quite a bit, you know, growing up. And through my life everything I've done has been a result of my dancing, my singing, [and] my culture. It's taken me, you know, all across the nation, overseas…."

Boye Ladd: ....."What I look for in a champion is the smoothness, the degree of difficulty in footwork, the speed, the beauty of his regalia (clothing), his ability to keep in time with the drum and your endings....

.....the various parts of each animal were incorporated into our regalia as well as the designs. Many of the designs you'll find today are out of respect to tribal affiliation or clan membership or perhaps a dream or a vision....

With the advent of the white man and a lot of the materials they brought with them, the needle and the use of metal, seed beads, porcelain, many of these things were added onto what we call the traditional format of structuring and making things out of beauty. The fluorescent colors are very bright so naturally [they] would get the judge's attention, [and] catch their eye as they come [came] spinning by.

Long ago you could identify a dancer by looking at his regalia and knew what tribe he came from. You look at our regalia; a lot of it might not necessarily be traditional as it is being-becoming more Pan American. In other words, everyone copies from one another, borrows from one another."

(*Schemitzun* by Kenneth A. Simon www.simonpure.com)

CEREMONIES

What I write here about ceremonies, the knowledge was gained mostly over the Internet. My source of information is the Iroquois Indian Museum just off Route 88 near Schenectady, NY. And it's very limited as the Iroquois are a private people who won't share information about some of their dances and most of their ceremonies. I respect that, but I can only relay printed information to you and how factual it is I can't attest to:

Cycle of Thanksgiving

Midwinter	January to February	*Ganaha'owi*	"Stirring the ashes"
Maple	February		Forest Dance
Maple Dance	March	*Hadichisto'ndas*	"Putting in Syrup"
All Night Dance	March-April	*Ohkiweh*	Honor the Ancestors
Thunder Dance	April		Arrival of Our grandfathers, the Thunderers
Hadueh	April		Medicine Mask Society

Seed Blessing	May	*Ganeha'ongwe dedwa'ye*	"Our seeds be better"
Moon Dance	May		Give thanks to Grandmother Moon
Sun Dance	May		Give thanks to the Sun
Strawberry Dance	June	*Wainodayo*	Celebrate the ripening of the strawberry
Green Bean Dance	July	*Wainodetgowaso*	Give thanks for the 1st of the 3 Sisters
Small Green Corn	mid-August		
Green Corn Dance	Aug.-Sept.	*Honondekwes*	Give thanks for corn and squash
Medicine Mask	October		
Okiiweh	October		Feast for the Ancestors
Harvest Dance	October	*Doyonunneo quana deohaka*	"We put our substance away"
Gaiwiio			Code of Handsome Lake

www.midtel.net/~iroquois/ceremonies.htm

"....we have dances that we do when we are giving thanks to the Creator, those are special dances. We do not do them as entertainment....

Our ceremonies are usually according to the moon....and all these things happen at certain moons, and we plant at a certain moon. And we give thanks for the seeds at a certain moon. Some of our ceremonies begin and end with the shortest days and the longest days of a year. And we don't have a 'new year' and we don't celebrate Christmas. But our people know of Christmas, and for that reason, sometimes if that certain moon for midwinter ceremony becomes close to Christmas, we move it back to the next moon, because they say that the earth is too noisy then. So the Creator may not hear us."

(Pulse of the Planet www.pulse.igc.org/archive/Aug00/2220.html)

CHAPTER SEVENTEEN

ORIGINS

From time-to-time, we all experience set-backs in our lives when the day just doesn't go like you think it should. This was one of those days.

Several months ago either on the PBS or the National Geographic network, a show was aired over several days on the origin of mankind. The project followed Dr. Spencer Wells from Africa to the Amerind tribes of the Southwest, more specifically, the Navajo. The show was sponsored by National Geographic and IBM. I not only watched every episode but I was able to borrow the DVD from our local library to view at my leisure, at home.

This was beneficial in that I could pause the story to take notes at critical points. The National Geographic team led by Dr. Wells followed genetic markers from a very remote tribe in Africa to the Navajo tribe in the Southwest. Speculation being that during the Ice Age there existed a natural land bridge through the Bering Strait allowing those hardy enough to be in that region, to cross to another continent.

I thought then that I could possibly do a link-up with Northeastern tribes, more specifically the Onondagas. This would help in establishing them in this region within a certain time-frame.

It is explained that a kit is available for purchase for a male that wants to trace his origin by mtDNA analysis. The kit is for men only because of the XY chromosome, (women have XX).

In any event, I had asked a gentleman on the Onondaga Reservation for his assistance in this project. I told him about the program many months before and gave him sufficient time to ponder it. I explained that it is a scientific approach to origins and has nothing to do with their religious beliefs.

Others on the Reservation, including his sister, had told me the story of Sky-woman (their religious story). David Cusick, an Onondaga, even wrote about it. I try very hard not to get into conversations about religion or political matters because I've observed that the opposing parties usually get heated-up over nothing. I respect others views and beliefs, and I hope that they do the same.

Anyhow, he called my house not long ago and told me that he had given the project some consideration and would be willing to do the testing. Based on that, I contacted National Geographic, placed an order and paid for an anonymous kit. I brought it to him yesterday and explained what he had to do to maintain accurate results. It involves scraping the lining of the inside of your mouth followed by the other cheek eight hours later. The kit is bar-coded and there is no identity as to whose DNA is being submitted. The same features apply to the shipping container—totally anonymous. They request that you not drink hot beverages on the day of the test as it has a tendency to destroy cells.

A call from him this morning set my research back, thoroughly confused me, and gave me a feeling of loss. He had approached the chiefs about the test and apparently they were upset. His reaction to this prompted him to call me and cancel the testing. Not only does this set my research back, but I feel that he doesn't trust me, which really hurts. I had explained the day before that the test was to be totally anonymous. The tubes and packaging were identified only by a bar-coded series of numbers. I had also explained that his name would not appear anywhere in my book.

I have shared ideas with this man for some three years now but I question if dialogue is important any longer if mutual trust is absent. I am willing to meet anyone half way to establish a friendship. The book research set-back doesn't bother me, but the friendship was cherished.

I have thought long and hard about what I might have said or done. It was said to me that the testing is just another way for the Federal Government to have information about them. This is totally ludicrous. I tried to reinforce the confidentiality of the tests but he had been told by higher authorities to forget it. There the conversation ended and I sensed not to pursue it further.

I guess that they have been hurt and mistreated so many times over the years that the paranoia is still ever present.

In looking back on my own heritage, I could have relayed to him the conflicts over the years between the United States and Canada regarding my Canadian heritage, such as the War of 1812. I could have explained that the Amerinds were not the only people to have major disputes with the British. My earliest ancestors were from Scotland and Ireland and we all know that they both fought the British over many long years. Clan leaders were killed, women raped, and land was taken away. But, life goes on. You shouldn't dwell on the past because you won't appreciate today and it will cloud your judgment about tomorrow.

As I reflect on the situation now, they are the ones who are losing vital information for the future. They have land claims (land rights) being reviewed by the courts as this goes to press. Wouldn't the established dates of say 13,000 to 14,000 documented years of occupancy be stronger for their case than 1,500 to 2,000 years attested to by early settlers, who are no longer around to back-up their statements or verify dates?

He walked away into the other room so I deduced that the conversation was over and I left. I'm sure that I'll see him again at lacrosse games in the future, but something in the building blocks of mutual trust is lacking some mortar. I shall try again with someone different, definitely not an Onondaga warrior.

I approached a Mohawk a few days later about the testing and he initially seemed willing but after a few days he sent me an e-mail explaining that the results would be far more accurate with a Cayuga or a Seneca, reason being that they were the last to be exposed to early white settlers and possible cross-breeding. They are located on the western edge of New York and the blood lines would probably be more pure.

The next step was to approach a Seneca acquaintance and his reaction left me absolutely astounded. "Why are you trying to stir things up, don't you know that the Seneca have *always* lived in this area. My ancestors have *always* been Seneca, are now, and *always* will be. We *never* came from another part of the world. We have *always* lived here. I have other things to do, if you'll pardon me."

I am wondering exactly where his people lived during the Ice Age when his territory was under the Wisconsin Ice Shelf which, I've told you, was more than a mile high. How could they possibly have lived in this region with no liquid water, no food, and no shelter? They must have migrated here as the ice receded and lakes began to form. Archeological dig sites and carbon dating attest to that. Why do they feel threatened? I don't want to change them but give them new information to ponder.

This is a very educated man and I'm perplexed by his response. Anyway, I will press on to accomplish my project, with or without them. There's obviously no cooperation on this, the paranoia is still ever present today that we whites have an ulterior motive. I can't change that. I thought I was trusted but I'm too naïve, I guess. I'll have to rely on modern-day scientific results.

In this regard, I do, however, want to share excerpts from an important paper titled, *"Mitochondrial DNA 'clock' for the Amerinds and its implications for timing their entry into North America."*

"ABSTRACT....Students of the time of entry of the ancestors of the Amerinds into the New World are divided into two camps, one favoring an 'early' entry [more than approximately 30,000 'years before the present' (YBP)], the other favoring a 'late' entry (less than approximately 13,000 YBP). An 'intermediate' date is unlikely for geological reasons.....we consider the mtDNA variation observed in 18 Amerind tribes widely dispersed throughout the Americas and studied by ourselves with the same techniques, and we estimate that if the Amerinds entered the New World as a single group, that entry occurred approximately 22,000-29,000 YBP.....The American Indians present a remarkable case study in human evolution. They belong to one of the few extant human groups whose ancestors entered a vast uninhabited area over a relatively short interval and then apparently remained isolated from other contacts for a considerable period of time.

Although there is consensus that their provenance was Eastern Siberia, the diversity of opinions on the exact time or times of the earliest human entry into the Americas has often been accompanied by acrimonious debate. As a broad generalization, the discussants of the 'entry problem' favor either an 'early' arrival [more than ≈ 30,000 years before present (YBP) or a 'late' arrival (less than ≈ 13,000 YBP)]

Studies of variation in mitochondrial DNA (mtDNA) offer a new approach to this long-standing question. Within the past 8 years, we have described mtDNA variation in 16 Amerind tribes. [We reserve the term Amerind for the descendants of the first wave or waves of immigrants to the New World, accepting for now that there was a later wave or waves of immigration, the ancestors of the Na-dene speakers and the North American Eskimos.]

DISCUSSION:

The average estimate for the arrival of the Amerinds resulting from the data now available is between 22,414 and 29,545 YBP.....

(Amerind migrations/Chibcha time depth/Amerind mtDNA evolution

Antonio Torroni, James V. Neel, Ramiro Barrantes, Theodore G. Schurr and Douglas C. Wallace

Department of Genetics and Molecular Medicine and Anthropology, Emory University, Atlanta, GA 30322; Department of Human Genetics, University of Michigan Medical School, Ann Arbor, MI 48109-0618; and *Escuela de Biologia, Universidad de Costa Rica*, San Jose, Costa Rica.

Proc. Natl. Acad. Sci. USA

Vol. 91, pp.1158-1162, February 1994

It is a quite lengthy and technical paper but is available for your viewing on the Internet under the key word—"Amerinds."

This from the *NATIONAL GEOGRAPHIC*—March 2006 "The Greatest Journey Ever Told—the Trail of Our DNA":

"The genes of people today tell of our ancestors' trek out of Africa to the far corners of the globe.

For decades the only clues were the sparsely scattered bones and artifacts our ancestors left behind on their journeys. In the past 20 years, however, scientists have found a record of ancient human migrations in the DNA of living people. 'Every drop of blood contains a history book written in the language of our genes', says population geneticist Spencer Wells, a National Geographic explorer-in-residence.

The article goes on to say that 'the genetic code, or genome, is 99.9% identical throughout the world. What's left is the DNA responsible for our individual differences—in eye color or disease risk, for example—as well as some that serves no apparent function at all.'"

After all is said and done there are some Native Americans that really are interested in their "genetic genealogy." You can pull up www.DNAAncestryProject.com The title of the program is Native American Ancestry which is powered by genebase. The cost for the genetic kit is $318.00 plus $25.00 for shipping. Mine, from National Geographic was $100.00 prepaid.

CHAPTER EIGHTEEN

AMERINDS-THE EARLY IMMIGRANTS

"The history of the Western Hemisphere is a history of immigration. Everyone, as far as we can know, came from somewhere else. There are no native Americans except that everyone born in the Western Hemisphere, is one. Among the American Indians (Amerinds), different groups went from Asia to the Western Hemisphere at different times, often centuries apart. And they continued to migrate, few stayed on the eastern end of the Bering Straits. Throughout the centuries, they migrated and then migrated again. We know that because there are variations in physical types. Height, color, hair, among other factors, varied a great deal.

> Blood type evidence supports the theory that they crossed a Bering Straits land bridge and supports their common origins, but there is also abundant evidence that people were in different places at different times. The Apache eventually invaded the territory occupied by the Zuni, for example. Iroquois-speaking nations were found not only in present-day New York and Canada but also in North Carolina, many hundreds of miles distant. Amerinds

acted much like the Africans, Asians, and Europeans did; they conquered each other.

Humans appear to be migratory creatures. First appearing in Africa, according to the best scientific evidence, different groups left Africa and settled in Europe and Asia and, eventually, in the New World. Science and some religions tell us that all human beings are cousins, that they all have at least one common grandparent.

It is only egotism or ignorance or both that causes humans and their progeny to see themselves as unique or different. But they did and do." (Donald J. Mabry www. historicaltextarchive.com —pg. 1)

I, myself, have always gravitated to the cultures of the Scottish and the Irish primarily because that is all I heard about from my parents and relatives or was exposed to while growing up. Come to find out, my direct lineage is to the Norwegian Vikings.

While writing this book I wanted to be one of the 100,000 men worldwide who were being tested by their DNA for their heritage link. I had heard that the islands off the coast of England were invaded a long time ago and my research indicates that in 795 AD the Irish areas of Dublin, Limerick, Mulligan, Wexford, Waterford, and Leixlip were invaded and pillaged. There were many large bases of operation for the Vikings from 830 to 1014 AD and intermarriages were common over this period of time.

In the relatively same geographic area, the Scots were also invaded about 836 AD. The Norwegian Vikings invaded Scotland, Shetland, Orkney, Caithness, and Sutherland. So it's a no-brainer that the strong Viking influence is there in my DNA. No wonder I liked hiking in the fjords of Norway in 1958. If I had known who my relatives were I could have stopped in for breakfast (tie-in to my first book-*My Time*).

"For 30,000 years people had been coming to the Western Hemisphere, taking what they wanted and having it taken from them in return. They negotiated to get what they wanted and fought for it, or both. They were [both] kind and cruel to each other. Some of them raped and pillaged and murdered. They moved around spreading from the eastern shores of the Bering Straits southwards to Tierra del Fuego at the tip of South America.

They bore children and their children bore children who bore children. Eventually some of these children left the ancestral area and became 'different people,' forgetting or not knowing that they were cousins to their rivals. For unknown reasons, some remained migratory, some farmed to supplement the food supply, and some built significant civilizations which had large buildings, complex social systems, and the pattern of imposing their will on their neighbors. In short, they were people acting as people act.

A new wave of immigrants, Europeans, started coming in the late 15th century; in many ways, this migration was part and partial of Western Hemisphere history....They imposed their food, ideas, clothing, political practices, and such on others.

The Europeans did have the advantage of having millions of allies to help them in their conquest. People tend to ignore these allies, 'microbes', even though they were the major force in the conquest. Disease is not heroic." (Donald J. Mabry www.historicaltextarchive.com —pg. 11)

The invasion of North America by the Whites, in a manner so markedly similar to those of the Indo-European invasions of Europe and other parts of the world thousands of years before, caused natural dissent from the inhabitants in the new territories.

Unlike the ancient Indo-Europeans, however, the Amerinds of America were not of distantly related genetic stock, as were the Old Europeans: they were of Mongoloid racial stock, only called "Indians" because the first white explorers were looking for India; and only called "red" because of their habit of wearing red clay as face paint.

The first meetings of Whites and Amerinds was mixed: generally the Amerinds were in awe of the technological wonders the Whites brought with them-starting with the ships themselves, which, with their billowing sails appeared like great spirits on the horizon: more than one instance is recorded of Amerinds fleeing in panic at the very sight of a White explorer ship. If they were in awe of the ships themselves, it needs no imagination to perceive what they must have thought of the wonders from the White world: clothes, steel, guns, mirrors, jewelry, copper, brass kettles and thousands of other things completely unknown to the native peoples of North America.

......The first horses were introduced to the continent by the Spanish: somehow a number escaped and by natural breeding formed large packs of wild horses which roamed the plains of America for nearly two centuries.

Finally, the new arrivals were not only light complexioned, but many of them also had beards and they all grew facial hair: this in itself was a subject of wonder by the Amerinds, who in their pure racial form did not grow facial hair at all, like their Mongolian cousins across the Bering Straits in Asia.

......two traits for which the Amerinds became known and for which they also became particularly disliked-were:

- The practice common amongst all the tribes of North America of cutting off the scalps of their vanquished foes to take as trophies for display in the tribal village. The appearance of White scalps —with blond, red, brown, or dark brown hair- were particularly prized, being outstanding compared to the pitch black haired scalps the Amerinds were more commonly used to taking from each other; and
- In common with their racial cousins in Central and South America, ritualistic cannibalism was common. The full extent of these practices was noted by many early writers, with the most complete and detailed account of Amerind cannibalism and the habit of torturing White prisoners of both sexes appearing in the print in 1892 in *The Works of Francis Parkman*, published by Little Brown, Boston (Vol. III.)

CHAPTER NINETEEN

DIET

I want to move on to the more common practices of the hunter/gatherers, that being, hunting wild game as early as the wooly mammoth, the mastodon, bears, panthers, Virginia deer, and various small mammals. There appear to have been plentiful amphibians and varieties of fish, as well. It was not uncommon for the tribes, in times of great hunger, to eat their dogs. The dog was around before the horse as a beast of burden pulling two-pole platforms as the tribes moved to other camp-grounds. Dogs were also used for hunting. To be eaten, the dog probably was sick or injured, or the people very hungry as these animals were highly valued.

In talking about Iroquois food, the prominence is placed on the Three Sisters—Corn, Squash, and Beans. I capitalize these three words to empathize their importance to the tribes. This terminology originated with the Iroquois even though other Amerinds eat from these food groups. Corn was the central plant with seeds planted fairly close together so there was strength and support in the stalks as they grew. Around the stalks were planted the beans so they could climb the stalks (a sort-of living trellis) and give more strength as they wound around. They also provided nitrogen. Adding shade and maintaining moisture for the roots were the squash plants. The vines of the squash plants contain prickly spines and hairs that help to keep marauding animals away. The mound of seeds and plants eventually became one foot high and two feet wide. This is called companion planting. www.landscaping.about.com

CHAPTER TWENTY

LIVING NATUARALLY

T oday's farmers can learn much from the Amerinds but they choose their own path. I have a small amount of fruit trees in my yard and two bee hives. An Onondaga gentleman suggested that I shouldn't spray the fruit trees, for two reasons: One, was that the residual spray would kill the bees trying to pollinate the fruit and the other was the toxicity of the airborne spray would affect your lungs and the toxic film on the fruit has carcinogens. Read the labels or listen to those "who were here first."

The Iroquois also knew that the soil would maintain plants for only a certain period of time. They had to add compost and fertilizer (nonexistent as they didn't have horses or cattle; but fish scraps were plentiful) or move on to a fresh plot of land.

You'll find that The People don't use chemicals on their property to control the spread of weeds or other undesirable plants. In our neighborhood, and probably yours too, there are companies that, for a fee, will spray your yard with chemicals to retard weed growth and insect infestation. You're paying a high price for this action. To my alarm, five housewives in our area contracted various forms of cancer. All five had their yards sprayed! Four died, one is in remission. This is not a scientific result, just my observation over the years.

I too am not immune to cancer. I experienced some discomfort in my neck this past summer. I was rinsing soap off my neck while taking a shower and felt a sensitive, tender spot. Since I hadn't fallen or bumped into anything I saw my doctor the following day to have it checked out. An ultrasound indicated a large mass in my neck. A biopsy a few days later confirmed my greatest fear. Surgery was called for and was scheduled as early as possible. The tumor proved to be malignant. I can't say for certain that the mist coming into our house through the windows from our neighbor's yard is the cause nor am I saying that it isn't!

Our area now has an ordinance against spraying on a windy day which would cause droplets to be carried to neighboring properties or through windows directly into homes. Such firms in violation are subject to fines or stronger actions. Our county is divided on this issue and a vote is to occur shortly. The other day an employee of one of these chemical firms had a brief discussion with me when I went next door to ask him if he would please stop the spraying.

He wasn't going to comply so I warned him that his next conversation would be with a Town of Manlius police officer while he was hand-cuffed, as I was going to press charges. I am that upset about what is going on. They now call two days before they're coming—better than nothing!

He tried to tell me that day that what he was doing was completely "harmless." I thought it was interesting that before he packed up and left, he placed yellow warning signs around the perimeter of the yard warning to keep pets and people off for 24 hours! If it's harmless, why the signs?

Well, I'll give you a scenario. Both pets and people will walk across the lawn and enter the house. The chemical residue is introduced on to your floors and carpeting. Infants crawl on the floor and pick up toys to play with which, more often than not, come in contact with their mouths. Older children lie on the floor while playing games or watching television. Dogs lick their feet and then also, showing affection, lick members of the family. Microscopic chemical droplets attach to dust particles which are then transported through the heating and air-conditioning ductwork in your homes. This then is taken into your lungs. Unwashed hands that have touched the pet or items picked up from the floor, touch food at the dinner table. Read enough?

The week of August 13th, 2007 I asked TRUGREEN-CHEMLAWN for a product listing of what is being sprayed on my neighbor's lawn. The gal at TRUGREEN-CHEMLAWN had actually called me to advise me that they would be spraying in our neighborhood in case I wanted to close windows and doors to keep away drift spray; and I asked for a listing of what is contained in that spray. The revised list of 1/01/07 which was mailed to me shows the following:

LESCO-PRE-M 3.3EC EPA Reg. No. 241-360-10404 (Pendimethalin) Warning label: **Keep Out of Reach of Children. There is a risk of chemical pneumonia or pulmonary edema**. This is caused by aspiration of the hydrocarbon solvent. **This is harmful if swallowed or absorbed through the skin. This product is toxic to fish**.

LESCO FERTILIZER PLUS 0.86% PRE-M EPA Reg. No. 10404-82 (Pendimethalin) **Keep Out of Reach of Children. Harmful if absorbed through the skin. This product is toxic to fish**.

DOW AGROSCIENCES TURFLON ESTER EPA Reg. No. 62719-258 (Triclopyr) **Keep Out of Reach of Children. Harmful if swallowed, inhaled, or absorbed through the skin. Avoid breathing mists or vapors. Avoid contamination of food. This product is toxic to fish.** (**Do not apply this product in a way that will contact workers or other persons, either directly or through drift. Avoid injurious spray drift**.)

RIVERDALE TRIAMINE II EPA Reg. No. 228-206 (Dimethylamine Salt of 2-Methyl-4-Chlorophenoxyacetic Acid) **Keep Out of Reach of Children. Harmful or fatal if swallowed. Harmful if inhaled. Avoid breathing spray mist. Do not get in eyes, or on clothing**.

RIVERDALE MCPA-4 AMINE EPA Reg. No. 228-143 (Dimethylamine Salt of 2-Methyl-4-Chlorophenoxyacetic Acid) **Keep Out of Reach of Children. Corrosive, causes irreversible eye damage. Avoid inhalation of mists. Harmful if swallowed, inhaled or absorbed through the skin. Do not apply this product in a way that will contact workers or other persons, either directly or through drift**.

BAYER TEMPO SC ULTRA EPA Reg. No. 432-1363 (Cyfluthrin, Cyano 4-fluoro-3-phenooxyphenyl methyl 3-2,2-dichloroethenyl 2,2-dimethylcyclopropanecar-boxylate) **Keep Out of Reach of Children. Harmful if absorbed through skin or inhaled. This product is extremely toxic to fish and aquatic invertebrates. Do not apply when weather conditions favor drift from treated areas**.

THE ANDERSONS-6.2% DYLOX EPA Reg. No. 9198-110

(Dimethyl) **Keep Out of Reach of Children. Harmful if swallowed, inhaled or absorbed through skin. Do not breath [breathe] dust. Vomiting should be induced if swallowed. This pesticide is toxic to fish and wildlife and is extremely toxic to aquatic invertebrates. Do not apply when weather conditions favor drift from areas treated. Do not apply where run-off is likely to occur.**

BAYER MERIT 75 WSP EPA Reg. No. 432-1318 (Imidacloprid) **Keep Out of Reach of Children. Harmful if swallowed, inhaled or absorbed through the skin. Avoid breathing dust or vapor. This product is highly toxic to aquatic invertebrates.**

This report goes on and on so I won't bore you with all the details but I will list the remaining toxic chemicals so that you will have the overall sense of what I am talking about:

THE ANDERSONS FERTILIZER WITH MERIT INSECTICIDE EPA Reg. No. 3125-474-9198 (Imidacloprid)

SEDGEHAMMER TURF HERBICIDE EPA Reg. No. 81880-10163 (Halosulfuron-methyl)

MANAGE by MONSANTO EPA Reg. No. 524-465 (Halosulfuron)

ACCLAIM EXTRA HERBICIDE EPA Reg. No. 432-950 (fenoxaprop-p-ethyl)

ROUNDUP PRO by MONSANTO EPA Reg. No. 524-475 (Glyphosate)

TALSTAR O .069% PLUS FERTILIZER 20-2-6 EPA Reg. No. 279-3216-10404 (Bifenthrin)

ZENECA HERITAGE FUNGICIDE EPA Reg. No.10182-408 (Azoxystrobin)

ASTRO INSECTICIDE EPA Reg. No. 279-3141 (Permethrin)

BAYLETON 50 EPA Reg. No. 3125-491 (1-4 chlorophenoxy-3,3-dimethyl-1-1H-1,2,4-triazol-1-yl-2-butanone)

AZATIN XL PLUS EPA Reg. No. 70051-27 (Azadirachtin)

TALSTAR ONE MULTI-INSECTICIDE EPA Reg. No. 279-3206 (Bifenthrin)

RIVERDALE TRI-POWER SELECT HERBICIDE EPA Reg. No. 228-262 (Dimethylamine Salt of 2-Methyl-4-Chlorophenoxyacetic Acid)

NOVARTIS BANNER MAXX FUNGICIDE EPA Reg. No. 100-741 (Propicanazole)

RAZOR PRO HERBICIDE EPA Reg. No. 228-366 (Bifenthrin)

TRIPLET LOW ODOR PREMIUM SELECTIVE HERBICIDE EPA Reg. No. 228-409 (Triisopropanolamine Salt of 2,4-Dichlorophenoxyacetic Acid)

BARRICADE 65WG HERBICIDE EPA Reg. No. 100-834 (Prodiamine n3.n3-Di-n-propyl-2,4-dinitro-6-ftifuoromethyl-m-phenylenediamine)

MATTCH BIOINSECTICIDE EPA Reg. No. 55638-47 (A blend of CrylAc and Crylc) ?

M-PEDE INSECTICIDE/FUNGICIDE EPA Reg. No. 62719-515 (Potassium salts of fatty acids)

LESCO WEED AND FEED 23-0-8 EPA Reg. No. 228301-10404 (2-Methyl-4-Chlorophenoxyacetic Acid)

DENDREX EPA Reg. No. 64014-1 (Acephate)

LESCO HORTICULTURAL OIL INSECTICIDE SUPERIOR OIL SPRAY EPA Reg. No. 10404-66 (refined petroleum distillate)

VALENT ORTHENE TURF TREE AND ORNAMENTAL SPRAY EPA Reg. No. 59639-26 (Acephate)

HEXYGON DF OVIDIDE/MITCIDE EPA Reg. No. 67545-AZ-1 (Hexythiazox)

LESCO WEED AND FEED 18-0-9 EPA Reg. No. 228-281-10404 (Dimethylamine Salt of 2,4-Dichlorophenoxyacetic)

DOW AGROSCIENCES CONSERVE SC TURF AND ORNAMENTAL INSECT CONTROL EPA Reg. No. 62719-291 (Spinosyn) *** **This product is highly toxic to bees exposed to spray. Avoid use when bees are actively foraging**. *** (which is April through November; otherwise, there is snow on the ground)

CAVALIER Flowable EPA Reg. No. 1001-69-10404 (Thiophanate-methyl dimethyl 4, 4'-o-phenylenebis 3-thioallo-phanate)

SURFLAN A.S. SPECIALTY HERBICIDE EPA Reg. No. 70506-44 (oryzalin:3,5-dinitro-N4N4-dipropylsulfanilamide) **Toxic to fish**.

MERIT 2 INSECTICIDE EPA Reg. No. 3124-418 (Imidacloprid, 1-6-Chloro-3-pyridinyl methyl-N-nitro-2-imidazolidinimin2)

FLORAMITE SC/LS-ORNAMENTAL MITICIDE EPA Reg. No. 400-509 (Bifenazate)

THE ANDERSONS FERTILIZER WITH BARRICADE HERBICIDE EPA Reg. No. 9198-123 (Prodiamine N3, M3-Di-n-propyl-2,4-dinitro-6-trifluoromethyl-m-phenylendi-amine)

RIVERDALE RAZOR HERBICIDE EPA Reg. No. 228-366 (Glyphosate, N-phospho-nomethyl glycine, in the form of its isopropy-lamine salt)

QUICK SILVER IVM HERBICIDE EPA Reg. No. 279-3272 (Carfentrazone-ethyl: Ethyl a,2-dichloro-5-4 difluoromethyl-4, dihydro-3-methyl-5-oxo-1H-1,2,4-triazol-1-yl-4-fluorobenzenepropanoate)

BUENO 6 EPA Reg. No.61483-15 (Monosodium Acid Methanearsonate)

RIVERDALE WEEDESTROY AM-40 AMINE SALT EPA Reg. No. 228-145 (Dimethylamine Salt of 2,4-Dichlorophenoxyacetic Acid) **Causes irreversible eye damage. Avoid inhaling vapor or spray mist.**

BARRICADE 4fl EPA Reg. No. 100-1139 (Prodiamine)

DOW AGROSCIENCES EAGLE 20EW EPA Reg. No. 62719-463 (Myclobutanil:a-butyl-a-chlorophenyl-1H-1,2,4, triazole-1-propanenitrile)

And lastly,

ANDERSONS TURF FERTILIZER 28-0-4 With Dicot Weed EPA Reg. No. 2217-794-9198 (2,4-dichlorophenoxyacetic acid +RY2J2 methyl-4-chlorophenoxy proplonic acid)

Source: (TRUGREEN—CHEMLAWN Product Information List –State of New York) Revised: 1-01-07

All have a warning to keep children away. Most post warnings of hazards to humans and domestic animals. Most are harmful if swallowed, breathed, or touched. Most are harmful to fish and aquatic animals.

I thank you for bearing with me, but the exposure of these chemicals is most important to me and to Native Americans today. We are using way too many chemicals in our environment just to have weed-free lawns and walkways. What kind of legacy are we passing on to subsequent generations? I don't have the knowledge as to whether these chemicals eventually break down (half-life), if ever, nor can I say with certainty that they have a carcinogenic potential. I'm a writer, not a chemist.

I personally am surrounded by these chemicals. Neighbors to the right and left of me as well as directly behind me, all use these applications in some form or another. Two of the six neighbors are medical doctors! One neighbor is in cancer remission and even has her house externally sprayed for insects every year.

I had cancer surgery on October 4, 2007 for an extremely large tumor in my neck. Guns and knives are in the city, dangerous chemicals in the suburbs. I rest my case.

* * *

This account is from the Jesuit, Father Lamberville in 1682: "On my arrival, I found the Iroquois of this village occupied in transporting their corn, their effects, and their cabins to a place 2 leagues * distant from their former residence, where they had dwelt for 19 years. They made this change in order to have firewood in convenient proximity, and to secure fields more fertile than those they were abandoning. This is not done without difficulty; for, inasmuch as carts are not used here, and the country is very hilly, the labor of the men and women, who carry their goods on their backs, is consequently harder and of longer duration.

To supply, with the lack of horses, the inhabitants of these forests render reciprocal aid to one another, so that a single family will hire sometimes 80 or 100 persons; and they are, in turn, obliged to render the same service to those who may request it from them, or they are freed from that obligation by giving food to those whom they have employed. [*Jesuit Relations* 62:55-57] (Tuck pgs.3-4) *1 league=5.556 kilometers

"Food remains, of both animal and plants, often comprised a part of our archaeological discoveries at Iroquois towns. Wild plants utilized by the Onondaga and mentioned by early visitors include blackberries, strawberries, grapes, plums, cranberries, mayapples, chestnuts, walnuts, probably hickory nuts, and the "universal plant", a medicinal, probably sassafras [*Jesuit Relations* 43:147, 257-59; 47:75]

"Since the dawn of time plants have been a sacred connection to Mother Earth. Plants feed, cure, and provide shelter. Throughout the world people have gathered herbs and spices, resin and roots to offer to the spirit world. Native traditions relate that wherever sage and cedar are used, no evil influences may enter. Herbs should be gathered in an ecologically sound and respectful way. The plants are not harmed and nothing is wasted." (Cherokee Sachem)

"Corn was first domesticated by Native American people over 6,000 years ago, in that part of North America today called Mexico. These early farmers shared their knowledge as well as seeds with other Native peoples, and corn-based agriculture spread as far south as Peru, and as far north as New York and Ontario. Corn began to be planted around 500 AD. It was just one of several plants cultivated here.

When the Iroquois homelands were intact, the job of growing the corn was carried out mainly by women. Iroquois men began farming only after being confined to reservations and reserves.

Corn exists today, not just as a plant, but also as a symbol. It stands for Iroquois identity. It stands for life. And it stands for spirit. The main Iroquois foods made with corn today include corn soup and corn bread." (www.iroquoismuseum.org)

You can obtain corn bread recipes by going to the Iroquois Museum web-site at www.iroquoismuseum.org/corn.htm. The museum is located near Albany, NY off Route 88 and is open from April 1st through December 31st. I actually like it better than the NA Museum in Washington, DC.

As a take-off on this, the Onondagas have a rock band with the name "Corn Bred" (raised on corn). I just thought I'd give them a plug, as they're incredible musicians, "Waterman, you owe me." They are the winners of the 9th Annual Native American Music Awards for the Best in Blues category.

On bass: John "J.B." Buck, on guitar: Morris Tarbell and Jerome Lazore, on drums: Lenny Printup, and on harmonica: non other than Curtis Waterman! They have their own web-site at www.cornbred.com where you can read their history and see their credits. But, what's important is that you must *hear* them! They are a traditional Native American sound with strong blues and rock influence.

CHAPTER TWENTY-ONE

THREE SISTERS-
THREE BROTHERS

I attended the commemoration program in Canandaigua for The Treaty of Canandaigua signing this past fall. At the luncheon, I overheard a conversation regarding Three Sisters versus Three Brothers. I knew that corn, squash, and beans were one part but I hadn't heard about the brothers. It was explained to me that the brothers are Burger King, Kentucky Fried Chicken, and McDonalds.

This leads to a small amount of research done by me on type 2 diabetes in Amerinds. I haven't been in close contact with the Onondagas for more than, I would say, 7 years. In that brief period of time I have observed that the Iroquois women and some of their children have a major weight problem. Native Americans used to eat a healthy diet and were probably more active with outdoor activities. They, like some of my Japanese friends, have developed a liking for fast food.

"Testing was done on Native Americans and Alaska Natives between 1990 and 1997 and was identified by the IHS (Independent Health Service) from a national output database. Within these years of 1990 to 1997, the number of Native Americans of all ages with diagnosed diabetes, increased from 43,262 to 64,474 individuals. Prevalence among women was higher than that among men. Prevalence by region was 3% in Alaska compared to 17% in the Atlantic region." (Diabetes Care, Vol.23, Issue 12, copyright 2000 American Diabetes Assoc.)

Prevalence of Diabetes among Native Americans and Alaska Natives, 1990-1997: An increasing burden by NR Burrows, LS Geiss, MM Engelgan, and KJ Acton—Headquarters Diabetes Program, Independent Health Service, Atlanta, GA nmrO@cde.gov

CHAPTER TWENTY-TWO

SUGAR IN THE BLOOD

Native American Diabetes Project
"Through the Eyes of the Eagle"

The story is told through the eyes of the eagle. The eagle represents strength, courage, and wisdom:

"This is the land of my Native people. As I soar high above through the clouds, I see the beauty of Mother Earth that she provides for my people, from the high peaks of the mountain tops, where the rivers begin, to the valleys below where the waters run through. I see Brother Sun as he greets each day with his morning light and I see him fade, to make room for Sister Moon.

As each day comes, the bear, the cougar, the deer, and I see the children, so pretty with a tan of golden brown, playing and running in their communities. The men with their legs so strong as to keep up with the antelope as they run. The women so beautiful as they work in the fields, as they grow all the things that make their families so healthy.

I remember when running was a way of life for everyone and so was living off Mother Earth with what she provided. Times were hard, but the Native People all worked together and shared in their labors and good fortunes through many feasts and celebrations. People came from far and near to join them in giving thanks to the Great Spirit for all that they were given and for a long, healthy life.

Brother Sun and Sister Moon have come and gone many times as I continue to fly over the land of my Native People. As each passing day goes by, I have seen many changes, some good and some bad. Mother Earth is still the same, for she continues to provide the nourishment for all living things, large and small. And also for the beauty that she provides for all to see and enjoy.

But, I now feel troubled and sad that I no longer see my Native people enjoying what Mother Earth has for them. With changing times, their labors are still hard but I see them not as strong as they could be. Modern days have brought about many changes where my people no longer run like the antelope. Children seldom play but watch what they call television. My people are getting sick by threes and fours with this thing called "Too Much Sugar in the Blood."

My Native People of golden brown no longer have the strength of their ancestors. As I soar through the clouds, I now see my people no longer active.

They suffer from lost vision and strength. Their feet, that once carried them over the lands of their birth, suffer great pain. Some of my people of golden brown now use wheels to get around. And others need machines to keep their bodies clean.

Oh, what a sad vision that my eyes now see. If only there was some way to give my people of golden brown my courage and strength to turn this around.

As I come to rest on my mountain top, I close my tired eyes of what I have seen and begin to see another vision of how it can be to bring back the strength and courage and long life to my people of golden brown.

My Native People are getting out and around. Slowly they come out by ones and twos to work and enjoy the riches and beauty that Mother Earth gives. They are walking and beginning to run and slowly get stronger as their sugars come down. As others see them getting stronger, they too want the same, so they join in until all are doing the same. They once again talk and share their ideas of what they can do to continue to grow healthier too.

They begin slowly by making one change, then two, to eat less sugar and less fat things too. As they get stronger and continue to make these changes, they come to know that they are healthier, not only in body but in mind and spirit too, as they now can control this thing called "Too much Sugar in the Blood."

Their children and grandchildren now know what they can do to grow and become stronger and healthier, too. By learning, and through examples taught by their parents and grandparents, they have obtained the wisdom of knowing what they need to do to keep their sugars down and have a healthier lifestyle.

As a new day approaches with Brother Sun bringing his light, I no longer feel troubled for I know they will learn what they can do to make my vision at rest all come to pass. My Native people of golden brown will once again be healthy and strong as they make the necessary changes to turn things around and once again will be strong in body and spirit." www.laplaza.org/health/eaglestory.html

"Nationally and locally, Native American communities around the country are working through "Awakening the Spirit" to encourage Congress to continue funding diabetes education programs in tribal communities." www.diabetes.org

"While diabetes occurs in people of all ages and races, some groups have a higher risk for developing type 2 diabetes than others. Type 2 diabetes is more common in African Americans, Latinos, Native Americans, and

Asian Americans/Pacific Islanders, as well as the aged population." www.
diabetes.org/type-2

....nearly 9 out of 10 people with newly diagnosed type 2 diabetes are
overweight. www.diabetes.org/weightloss

"1940-today, Native Americans have a high risk for diabetes; "new
Western diet" blamed.

1998 $33 million appropriated by Congress for the Indian Diabetes
Project" www.Montana.edu/wwwai/imsd/diabetes

CHAPTER TWENTY-THREE

PRESENT DAY CONCERNS

T he major concerns for the Amerinds of Central and Northern New York appear to be the issues of casinos, taxation on retail sales of items sold on reservations (especially tobacco), land claims or land rights issues, sovereignty issues, and re-establishment of clean air and water.

Another issue is border crossings raised by the Mohawks on the reservations bordering the St. Lawrence River both on the Canadian and American sides.

A letter was sent out on 11/16/05 from Carrie Garrow, who is the Executive Director of the Center for Indigenous Law, Governance & Citizenship at the College of Law—Syracuse University and I quote:

"The United States government [sic] adopted the Intelligence Reform and Terrorism Prevention Act of 2004, which provides that by 2008 all U.S. citizens and non-immigrant aliens must possess a passport or some other form of proof of citizenship to cross back into the United States.

During September and October 2005, the federal government [sic] accepted comments on proposed rules regarding what other form of identification may be acceptable in lieu of a passport. The Center for Indigenous Law, Governance & Citizenship submitted comments stating that the U.S. government must accept proof of Indigenous citizenship because of our right, protected by the Jay Treaty, to cross freely back and forth across the border....Also, watch the news as the federal government [sic] will at some point make public it's new rules regarding what form of identification that will be acceptable to cross the border. We will be monitoring this issue closely and welcome your thoughts and comments."

My response:
Attn: Carrie Garrow and Chris Ramsdell

Dear Ladies,

Thank you for including my name in your mailing. I am not a member of the *Haudenosaunee* as I am a white male born and living in New York State. I possess a valid U.S. passport and have had one for many years since I've traveled out of the country. The purpose, you know, of passports or identity papers is to monitor who is coming into this country that shouldn't be here or that might pose a threat to our safety (yours and mine) due to the infamous day of 9/11/01.

Canada and the U.S. have a lengthy, virtually unprotected border that is impossible to monitor sufficiently at all times. The two governments feel that the days of unrestricted travel are history because of recent attacks. My suggestion, for whatever it's worth, would be to have your own bilingual passport similar to one that Oren Lyons uses when he travels. It should be partly in English so that the crossing guards can obviously read it. Perhaps the use of French could be added for those crossing at the Quebec border. A current photo would, of course, be helpful too.

These are hard times for all of us, Native or not, to have to cope with restrictions we're not used to having in the past.

My wife and her parents left this week for a business trip to Dallas which meant getting up very early in the morning because of long lines at the security area in the airport. My mother-in-law is restricted to a wheelchair and must WALK through the metal detector because of the steel frame of her wheelchair. There is no point in parking the car because you can no longer go to the departure gate with the passengers. The police are at the curb telling you to immediately move your car after unloading.

We are all scrutinized with two sets of eyes today but that's just what we have to get used to in the name of "safety".

I guess what I'm saying is that we're all in this together. My second daughter married a man who was born in Cairo, Egypt. What you and I have to put up with is nothing compared to what he goes through on a daily basis.

When the Jay Treaty was written way back in 1794, there wasn't a governor or *tadodaho* back then who could foretell what this world would experience.

If we remain calm and strive for the proper paperwork, it will, in the long run, benefit all of us.

Respectfully submitted, 11/16/05
Jack Edgerton

CHAPTER TWENTY-FOUR

LAND RIGHTS— CLEAN WATER— ECOLOGY ISSUES

UNITED STATES DISTRICT COURT
NORTHERN DISTRICT OF NEW YORK,
Plaintiff,

    -against-

CAROL M. BROWNER, as Administrator, and
United States Environmental Protection Agency
Defendants

STATE OF NEW YORK
COUNTY OF ONONDAGA

CHIEF IRVING POWLESS, JR. hereby declares under penalty of perjury pursuant to 28 USC 1746 as follows:

1. I am a Chief of the Onondaga Nation and I serve on the governing body of the Onondaga Nation: the Council of Chiefs. As such, I am familiar with the facts and circumstances pertaining to the Onondaga Nation's history as well as its traditions and culture for the preservation

of our natural resources, particularly our bodies of water, rivers, creeks and streams for the future use of the seventh generation yet to be born.

2. Make this Declaration, on behalf of the Onondaga Nation Council of Chiefs, in support of Atlantic States Legal Foundation, *et al.*'s civil action challenging the United States Environmental Protection Agency's issuance of a finding of no significant impact, in relation to the Midland Avenue combined Sewer Overflow Abatement Project.

3. The government of the Onondaga Nation has at all times been the Council of Chiefs, a governing body constituted since time immemorial according to the traditional law of the *Haudenosaunee*, referred to as the *Gayonishehgowa*, or the Great Law of Peace.

4. The council of Chiefs is and has, at all relevant times, been formally recognized by the government of the United States. As one of the Chiefs of the Onondaga Nation, I have the authority to attest to the actions and decisions of the Onondaga Nation and its Council of Chiefs. The Onondaga Nation Council of Chiefs, acting with the Clan Mothers, according to its traditional laws under the Great Law, is the only authority that determines the actions of the Onondaga Nation.

5. Onondaga Lake and its tributaries are located within the Onondaga Nation's historic, aboriginal, and sovereign land area.

6. The Onondaga Nation plans to continue the defense of its historic land claim.

7. Through the Onondaga Nation's land claim, the Onondaga Nation has a future interest in Onondaga Lake, Onondaga Creek, Ley Creek and Harbor Brook.

8. Each of these water bodies will be effected [affected] by the EPA's decision to relieve Onondaga County from its duty to prepare an [a] full environmental review of its general combined sewer overflow abatement program, and each of the plan's component parts, particularly the Midland Avenue Combined Sewer Overflow Abatement Project.

9. Prior to European immigration to the Onondaga Territory, the Onondaga Nation had villages throughout what is now known as Onondaga County.

10. As the European encroachment on the Onondaga Territory continued, throughout the eighteenth century, the Onondaga villages were pushed southward, up Onondaga Creek.

11. The Onondaga Nation settled on the banks and islands of Onondaga Creek, and were pushed further south, and forced to resettle our villages.

12. This resettlement and eviction process repeated itself several times until approximately 1825, when the Onondaga Nation established itself near the headwaters of Onondaga Creek, five miles south of Syracuse, New York.

13. There are vestiges of the prior Onondaga villages along Onondaga Creek. These former village sites are of great archeological and cultural importance to the Onondaga Nation.

14. The installation of one and one half miles of pipeline, with a diameter ranging from five to twelve feet, will disturb our ancient village sites and will also probably disturb many burial sites of our ancestors.

15. Future combined overflow projects along Onondaga Creek could disturb more of our ancient village sites and many more burial sites of our ancestors.

16. The Onondaga Nation was never approached, notified or consulted by Onondaga County regarding its plan to address combined sewer overflow problems through construction of pipelines and sewer treatment facilities along the banks of Onondaga Creek.

17. The Onondaga Nation was never approached, notified or consulted by the United States Environmental Protection Agency regarding Onondaga County's plan to address combined sewer overflow problems through construction of pipelines and sewer treatment facilities along the banks of Onondaga Creek.

18. The Onondaga Nation was never approached, notified or consulted by New York State's Historic Preservation Office regarding the archeological and historical significance of the Onondaga Creek corridor, in relation to Onondaga County's plan to address combined sewer overflow problems through construction of pipelines and sewer treatment facilities along the banks of Onondaga Creek.

Dated: March 9, 2000 _____

CHIEF IRVING POWLESS, JR.

Following is the text of the legal papers filed on March 11, 2005 regarding the Onondaga land rights issue filed at the Federal Court House in Syracuse, New York after which is the most appropriate response from Susan Lyons of the Onondaga Nation that I have read. I couldn't have said it with any more feeling than she expresses.

UNITED STATES DISTRICT COURT
NORTHERN DISTRICT OF NEW YORK
THE ONONDAGA NATION,

Plaintiff,

V.

THE STATE OF NEW YORK; GEORGE PATAKI, IN HIS INDIVIDUAL CAPACITY AND AS GOVERNOR OF NEW YORK STATE; ONONDAGA COUNTY; THE CITY OF SYRACUSE; HONEYWELL INTERNATIONAL, INC.; TRIGEN SYRACUSE ENERGY CORPORATION; CLARK CONCRETE COMPANY, INC.; VALLEY REALTY DEVELOPMENT COMPANY, INC.; HANSON AGGREGATES NORTH AMERICA

Defendants.

COMPLAINT FOR DECLARATORY JUDGEMENT

Nature of the Action

The Onondaga people wish to bring about a healing between themselves and all others who live in this region that has been the homeland of the Onondaga Nation since the dawn of time. The Nation and its people have a unique spiritual, cultural, and historic relationship with the land, which is embodied in *Gayanashagowa*, the Great Law of Peace. This relationship goes far beyond federal [Federal] and state [State] legal concepts of ownership, possession, or other legal rights. The people are one with the land and consider themselves stewards of it. It is the duty of the Nation's leaders to work for a healing of this land, to protect it, and to pass it on to future generations. The Onondaga Nation brings this action on behalf of its people in the hope that it may hasten the process of reconciliation and bring lasting justice, peace, and respect among all who inhabit this area.

This is an action to declare that certain lands are the property of the Onondaga Nation and the *Haudenosaunee*, having been unlawfully acquired by the State of New York in violation of the federal [Federal] Indian Trade and Intercourse Acts, now codified at 25 U.S.C. 177, and in violation of the United States Constitution, the Treaty of Fort Stanwix of 1784, and the Treaty of Canandaigua of 1794.

Jurisdiction and Venue

The jurisdiction of this court is invoked pursuant to 28 U.S.C. 1331, 1337, 1343, and 1362. Venue lies in this District under 28 U.S.C. 1391 (b).

Plaintiff's claim for relief arises under federal [Federal] common law; the United States Constitution; the Indian Trade and Intercourse Acts of 1790, 1793, 1796, 1799, 1802, and 1834, now codified at 25 U.S.C. 177; under the Treaty of Fort Stanwix of 1784, 7 Stat. 15; and the Treaty of Canandaigua of 1794, 7 Stat. 44.

Parties

The plaintiff ONONDAGA NATION is an Indian nation recognized by the United States through the Secretary of the Interior of the United States. It is, and has been at all relevant times, an "Indian nation" within the meaning of the federal [Federal] Indian Trade and Intercourse Acts of 1790 and later, now 25 U.S.C. 177. The citizens of the Onondaga Nation reside principally

111

on their territory or "reservation" south of Nedrow, New York. The Nation brings this action by authority of the Onondaga Council of Chiefs, the sole government of the Onondaga Nation. The government of the Onondaga Nation is recognized by the United States through the Secretary of the Interior. The relationship of the Onondaga Nation to the United States has never been terminated.

The Onondaga Nation sues on its own behalf and on behalf of and with the authority of the *Haudenosaunee*. The *Haudenosaunee* is a confederacy, originally, of five Indian nations: the Onondaga Nation, Mohawk Nation, Oneida Nation, Cayuga Nation, and Seneca Nation. The Tuscarora Nation joined the Haudenosaunee in approximately 1712. It is called, in English, the "Six Nations Iroquois Confederacy." The capitol or central Council Fire of the Confederacy is at Onondaga. The Onondagas are the fire keepers of the *Haudenosaunee*. The *Haudenosaunee* entered into two treaties recognized as valid by the United States: the Treaty of Fort Stanwix of 1784 and the Treaty of Canandaigua of 1794. This action is brought by authority of the Council of Chiefs of the *Haudenosaunee* as well as by authority of the Council of Chiefs of the Onondaga Nation. The *Haudenosaunee* does not object to this case proceeding in its absence.....

The continuance of legal papers goes on for many more pages and stresses 44 major points which you read for yourself at: www.indianlaw.org/pdf/dpa/onondaga/landclaimfiling2005

"To the Editor:

My real name is *Owenjunedu*, a member of the Onondaga Nation. I feel that for my own healing I must share the feelings I have regarding New York State's motion to dismiss our land rights action. I knew New York State would do this. I knew it was coming. I thought I was ready.

I realize now that deep down I did have some hope that this time they would be fair; that this time justice will be done and we could begin the healing of generations of trauma that all Native Americans in this country have endured and are still enduring.

I cried when I read in the papers New York State has filed a motion to dismiss. I cried and I felt a great sadness, not just for our youth and their future, but I felt the weight of years of sadness of my ancestors.

I felt that this unjust blow to our nation is no different than sending in the troops to destroy us, except this time the battle is in the courts, not in our homes.

This does not make it any less tragic or painful. I'm here to say that despite the sadness and this attempt to keep justice from us, we will continue our ways.

We will continue our ancient ceremonies of thanksgiving for all that the Creator has given us, and we will do this on behalf of all who inhabit this Earth, as we have for centuries. We will also continue to assert our sovereignty and our rights because like it or not, we are still here." Susan Lyons (*The Post Standard* Friday, September 1, 2006 pg. A-13)

**At the time of this writing, the Federal Government is making a determination as to whether it will join in the suit against New York State. **

CHAPTER TWENTY-FIVE

EDUCATION

"I am a living entity. The creator inspired my birth. Your thirst for the truth about yourself and Mother Earth will be within your reach when your spirit and mine are congruent. My truth will give you the strength and courage to exist in all cultures but it will also give you the ability to retain the intrinsic values of our way of life. Some day some of you will return to me and share with others what you have gained, both within me and in other entities similar to me, in our little brother's culture. The pride that I will generate in you and the way of life that I will give you, will place you high above all your enemies such as greed, envy, jealousy, resentment, self pity, anger, revenge, dishonesty, and egotism...If I live within you, you will be like the eagle."

(ONS philosophy)

In 1850 the Onondaga Indian School began in a one room schoolhouse. It was originally located on Kennedy Road on the far eastern border of the Nation. In 1910 it was moved to Route 11A into a two story house. The school then was K-6. In 1940 New York State erected part of the present brick structure and in 1950 it was expanded.

To further their education at the time, students would attend Roosevelt

Jr. High in the city and then move on to Central High School, Vocational H.S., or Onondaga Valley Academy. In earlier years, students attended the Hampton Indian School in Virginia, the Carlisle Indian School in Pennsylvania, the Haskell Indian School in Kansas, or the Thomas Indian School in Cattaraugus, NY.

In 1970 the community developed an Onondaga Language and Culture program as part of the curriculum. In 1995 major renovations were made again which included additional classroom space and a new gymnasium.

ONS, by the way, was recently recognized by the Board of Regents and the New York State Education Department as an Electronic Doorway Library. The children have access to SIRS Discover, Grolier Online, Yahooligans, Jeeves for Kids, Berit's Best Sites for Children, Awesome Library, CNN, Kid's Courier, Time for Kids, USA Today, Ranger Rick, and National Geographic for Kids to name a few.

At the high school level, at Lafayette H.S., the district implemented the Nova NET system to offer students free remedial online courses that will help students prepare for SAT and ACT courses. Paula Cowling, the high school principal, has this to contribute, "Most schools offer summer school as a way to make up failed classes. Some allow students to move to the next grade while making up the class; others retain the student. Lafayette's online program prevents kids from having to repeat courses or to be held back. This preserves the students' integrity. They can stay with their class and not be discredited by having to repeat. Kids love computers. This gives them a new way to learn, and another opportunity to be successful."

"The graduation rate [at Lafayette] in 2000 was 73%; in 2005 it dropped to 67%" It was the lowest for public schools in Onondaga County according to Superintendent Mark Mondanaro. It was time for a new approach.

The district also wants to launch a pre-K program at both the ONS and at Grimshaw Elementary." (Doran 7/23/07)

The present day Onondaga Nation School (ONS) on Route 11A, consists of the grades Kindergarten through 8th grade. The current enrollment is approximately 88 students of which 41 are girls, 47 are boys. On average there are approximately 9 to 10 students per grade. It is an incredibly beautiful, modern, up-to-date school which replaced the old school that, I heard, burned years ago. There is a playground, a library, tech room, gymnasium, lunch room, and a music room. The faculty is roughly 50% white, 50% Native American, the staff mostly Native American.

It is this music room that will always be on the minds of 17 young, Native American girls, their parents and relatives, the non-Native school nurse, the non-Native school librarian, and the non-Native principal, all of whom will play a part in the upcoming trial in July and August of 2007.

It was on a cold day in the month of *TISAH* (December) in the year 2006 that three very brave young girls decided that they had had enough of abnormal attention from their music teacher. They didn't want the younger girls in the school to be exposed to what they had endured the past few years. It was time to expose the monster in their midst.

The school nurse was the person to share this information with. She could be trusted and would certainly know what to do to make it stop.

The scope of the investigation (which included the interviewing of approximately 60 students), revealed that as many as 17 young girls out of 41 (nearly half) had allegedly been molested by the hands of their white music teacher over a period of several years.

It was time to take the statements of the young girls by the Onondaga County Sheriff's Department, place the teacher under arrest, and prepare for a trial in the white man's court. You see the ONS is part of the Lafayette School District and a trial for crimes of this magnitude would be held in County Court, in downtown Syracuse. Not since 1978 have the tribal chiefs and elders allowed justice to be determined off the reservation.

The Grand Jury weighed the evidence presented and heard the testimony of the girls and witnesses to determine that there was sufficient cause for a criminal trial. The defendant had his attorney; the girls had the District Attorney's Office and Vera House counselors to help get them through a scenario not familiar to them.

The security police directed me to the 3rd floor of the Court House. Part II which is the court of Judge Walsh, is in Room 320. The calendar showed the current trial in that hall of justice as INDICT #2007-0383-1, DR #06-488514 with the defendant's name, Al Scerbo. It is now toward the ending days of *SESKAGONAH* (July).

The representation of these young girls would be in the capable hands of Kari Armstrong and Gary Dawson of the District Attorney's Office, while Mr. Scerbo would have the experienced Ed Menkin as his lawyer. Due to my own medical problems, I was unavailable for the opening remarks and the first day of testimony.

The school nurse, I understand, was one of the first witnesses called to testify. I was able to hear her testimony, however, when the court transcriber read back her testimony during deliberation.

Subsequent days were gut-wrenching as each little girl was lead into the courtroom and told to sit next to the judge. He did his best throughout the trial to help them relax and maintain calm.

They very seldom come downtown much less walk into a building that appears so stark and cold; to have three white lawyers asking them very direct, personal questions. Next to them are seated jurors and alternates—people they don't know. Throughout the building and courtroom wander men and women police officers with guns at their hips.

"Now tell us Miss….. in your own words, where was his hand? Was it above your waist or below it? Was it on top of your skirt or under? Did he keep his hand still or did he move it? How did he move it? What do you call that part of your body? What is it used for?" On, and on, and on, the 2nd, 3rd, 4th, and 5th graders were asked these most embarrassing questions in front of total strangers.

My heart went out to them. When they cried, I cried. When they were angry, I was angry. Some could hardly testify at all—they were that frightened and intimidated. The inability of some to recall dates or to remember what exactly they testified to at the Grand Jury months before was construed as lying. Most of them wanted to forget what had happened and move on. The brain has ways of blanking out the horrific. The girls just wanted to play and laugh again!

When they left the courtroom crying with their moms, I was even angrier to see the anguish in their beautiful, little faces. A large chunk of their lives was ripped away by an alleged, serial, predator-pedophile. Their lives will never be the same all because of a teacher's alleged lust for little girls. When I see their parents at the next box lacrosse game, I'm not sure of what to say to make them feel better.

He should never have been teaching there as his racist feelings of "us vs. them" came out ever so strongly when he was on the stand. He also lied to previous employers, i.e. the school districts of Liverpool and Phoenix as well as the Lafayette district about his military background and rank. He was never a Staff Sergeant, was never in Special Forces, and was never a U.S. Army Ranger. So, on the stand under oath, what else might he have lied about?

Parts of the trial placed major emphasis on the years when the girls would have been in a certain grade and what part of the year did he bother them. Who cares? It's not important WHEN—but WHAT he did!

I want to let you know now that I am not a Native American so you'll better understand where I'm coming from. I am of Scottish-Irish lineage from a dad born in Canada. I do, however, consider my neighbors to the south to be true friends and I hope that those who know me on the "rez" feel the same. I came to the trial for three reasons: most importantly to offer support, secondly to gain valuable information for my book on the *Haudenosaunee*, and to empathize with and sympathize for, other grieving parents.

I was interviewed by a reporter from S.I. Newhouse School of Journalism at Syracuse University, who after reading the biased newspaper accounts (Post Standard, New York Times) himself, wanted a fair slant as to how the trial was proceeding. Having been on jury duty 4 times over several years (as I recall—2 criminal, 2 civil), I feel that I can see through the smoke-screen to determine the facts as they are presented.

I cast no ill feelings on the 12 jurors, but I heard and witnessed the trial as they did and I came to totally different conclusions. What did they not hear or see that I did? Had I been on the jury, the vote would have been different. But, they hopefully did the best they could. That is the system we have, be it good or bad.

Years ago when O.J. Simpson was acquitted, and more recently the actor, Robert Blake, I asked myself, "What's the sense of it all?" I hate to admit it but I had the same feeling this afternoon as I walked back to my car to go home. How do I tell my wife and daughters that he got away with too many crimes after discussing the ins and outs of the trial every night over dinner?

True, he'll probably serve prison time for the "GUILTY" that we heard on a few counts but I feel that his personal life at home, in the meantime, can't be maintained as before due to the shocking testimony that his wife and relatives heard about him day after day.

He now must register as a pedophile; must have supervised visits with his own children; and must appear at a trial in family court where both he and his wife face charges of child neglect. He more than likely will never teach again and he faces a possible 7 years in prison, according to the assistant district attorney, Mr. Dawson.

Today is the 2nd day of *KENTENAH* (August), the trial is over but the crying will continue long into the night on the reservation. I will be at the sentencing on the 10th of *CHUTOWAAH* (October), for sure. (I never made it as I had cancer surgery on the 4th and was recuperating at home.)

It certainly is not the first time that Native American school children have been mistreated at the hands of white teachers. I just finished the book titled, "Indian School—Teaching the White Man's Way" by Michael L. Cooper. In it he explores the Carlisle Indian Boarding School in Pennsylvania.

On October 6th, 1879, Captain Richard Henry Pratt arrived by train in Carlisle with several Native American boys and girls some of whom were the children of White Thunder, Red Cloud, and Spotted Tail. There were 84 in total, many of whom were sons and daughters of chiefs from different territories.

As the children were initially gathering to leave with Pratt, Red Cloud had the following to say, "The white people are all thieves and liars. We do not want our children to learn such things. The white man is very smart."

Pratt's response was, "….you cannot read or write. You cannot speak the language of this country…because you were not educated, these mountains, valleys, and streams have passed from you. Your ignorance against the white man's education will more and more hinder and restrain you and take from you." (Indian School pg. 3)

Many of the children were terrified before they even arrived at Carlisle as they were subjected to a lengthy ride (four days for some) on the "iron horse." Next was a walk from the train station to the campus which consisted of converted British army barracks built 130 years earlier.

Here they were not only leaving their families, but also a way of life. Native Americans, you see, were clinging desperately to their traditional ways as their population was rapidly declining. There were estimated to be more than a million Native Americans at the beginning of the nineteenth century to fewer than three hundred thousand in 1879. (Indian School pg. 19)

Some Indians went to Carlisle willingly while others were tricked into going or merely snatched away not to see their parents until several years later.

Life was not easy for any of them as they had to discard their clothing and moccasins to wear uniforms and shoes. The boys had to submit to short haircuts while the girls were allowed to keep their braids. The food served to them was totally foreign and that they had to sit on a chair at a table was most strange. A different language was forced on them and quite often they were reprimanded physically for speaking their own tongue. They also had to choose a new "Americanized" name or one would be assigned to them.

There is a cemetery at Carlisle as many Native children died there when exposed to the white man's diseases such as influenza for which they had no immunity. Homesickness also took its toll.

Natives excelled in sports at Carlisle especially the game of football. In 1912, a game featured two famous running backs. For Carlisle the name was Jim Thorpe, for Army the leadership fell to Dwight D. Eisenhower. "One of the team's biggest games was against West Point. Before they took the field, the quarterback recalled, 'Pop Warner (the Carlisle coach) had no trouble getting the boys keyed up for the game. He reminded the boys that it was the fathers and grandfathers of these Army players who fought the Indians.'

That was enough!" Army-6, Carlisle-27 (Indian School pgs.78-79)

"Native Americans who had been armed with the white man's education, like Zitkala-Sa and Charles Eastman, were able to defend themselves against ignorance and prejudice while helping to preserve their unique heritage." (Indian School pg. 92)

I found it most interesting the other day to read that the Lafayette District wants to start teaching the language of the Onondaga. It wasn't all that many years ago that a young Native boy or girl would be punished for speaking their tongue and not English—events come full circle if you wait long enough.

I received the following by e-mail from Sara Mortimer of Syracuse University News on August 25, 2006 and I thought I'd share it with you. It's a nice way to end my book on an encouraging and positive note:

"Syracuse University News—Tuesday, August 22, 2006

On August 15, 2005, members of the Syracuse University and *Haudenosaunee* communities announced a new scholarship program to provide qualified American Indian students with the necessary financial resources to attend S.U. It was announced that the *Haudenosaunee* Promise Scholarship Program, administered by the University Office of Scholarship Programs, would provide financial assistance equal to the cost of tuition, on-campus room and board, and mandatory university fees to all admitted first-year and transfer students who are certified current citizens of one of the six *Haudenosaunee* nations.

One year later, S.U. is pleased to be welcoming 44 Native American students to campus this fall, with 30 of these students—17 first-year and 13 transfer students— here as part of the *Haudenosaunee* Promise. Because of the Promise and other campus and outreach efforts, the Native American population of incoming students has grown eight-fold from 2004 to the greatest population size in S.U. history. This year, more than nine territories will be represented.

'I am delighted to welcome such a large group of bright and gifted students to the University,' says S.U. Chancellor and President Nancy Cantor. 'We are continuing to build and expand upon our historical relationship with the *Haudenosaunee*, and the results thus far are truly exciting.'

The Promise, developed to express S.U.'s gratitude and appreciation for the historical, political, and cultural legacies of the *Haudenosaunee*, financially assists qualified Native American students in each year of study toward their first bachelor's degree. Scholarship recipients are required to maintain full-time academic status at S.U.

with a minimum 2.5 cumulative grade point average. S.U. does not limit the number of Promise scholarships awarded annually.

'In having set out to make Syracuse University accessible to students of the *Haudenosaunee*, we are truly impressed with how well the first year has gone,' says David C. Smith, vice president for enrollment management. 'There is no question that we are on our way to a much higher level in our relationship.' Last year, [Nancy] Cantor named [David] Smith as the university's emissary to the *Haudenosaunee*, and Stephanie Waterman '83, G'04 was appointed the Onondaga Nation's emissary to the University.

To qualify, students must be citizens of one of the following territories throughout New York State and Canada that are part of the *Haudenosaunee* Nations: *Akwesasne* Mohawk, *Kantatsiohareke* Mohawk, *Ganienke* Mohawk, *Kahnawake* Mohawk, *Kanesatake* Mohawk, *Tyendinaga* Mohawk, Tonawanda Seneca, Six Nations (Canada), Oneida (New York), Oneida of the Thames (Ontario), Onondaga, Allegany Seneca, Cattaraugus Seneca, Oil Spring Seneca, and Tuscarora.

Lisa Parker of Akron, N.Y., and a member of the Tonawanda Seneca Nation, will be a freshman at S.U. as part of the *Haudenosaunee* Promise and [she] plans to study education. 'I feel that many of the obstacles that Native American students may face have been addressed currently through the *Haudenosaunee* Promise Scholarship,' says Parker. 'Syracuse University has provided students opportunities to alleviate cultural differences by providing academic and personal support, providing opportunities to meet and live in a Native American Learning Community residence hall, attend small group information sessions with family members before opening day, and opportunities to meet S.U. faculty and staff.

Odie Brant Porter, assistant provost at S.U. and also a citizen of the Seneca Nation (Allegany Territory) notes, 'This is an exciting time to witness the increase in the Native student population. Our Native students bring many distinct talents and perspectives, so the learning process will be mutually beneficial to both Natives and non-Natives alike.'

As a form of collaboration between academics and student life, the Division of Student Affairs Office of Multicultural Affairs (OMA) has established a new program to help all Native American students on campus. Named the Native Student Program, the initiative is led by Regina Jones, assistant director in OMA, and housed at 113 Euclid Ave. It is designed to help Native students transition into college life and access support throughout their career at S.U. The program launched August 1st and has partnered in hosting orientation events for new Native students.

Robert Odawi Porter, director of the College of Law Center for Indigenous Law, Governance, and Citizenship, notes that S.U.'s commitment to Native American students is like none other in higher education. 'No other university has made this kind of commitment to neighboring aboriginal people,' says Porter. 'For too long we have struggled to resist Western efforts to de-culture our people through education. Now, through Chancellor Cantor's leadership, S.U. is creating an opportunity for us to achieve a *Haudenosaunee* intellectual renaissance.' Porter is a citizen of the Seneca Nation of Indians and was raised on its Allegany Territory in Upstate New York.

In the past two years, the University has worked to expand its academic offerings in related areas. Richard Loder '67, G'78, part-time professor of sociology in the Maxwell School of Citizenship and Public Affairs, was appointed to a three-year directorate of the Native American Studies Program in the College of Arts and

Sciences, the first time a faculty member of Native American heritage has served in a leadership position in the college. Loder's appointment is part of a re-envisioning of the Native American Studies Program to expand its offerings to all members of the University community."

For more information on the Promise scholarships, contact Patricia Johnson, Office of Financial Aid and Scholarship Programs, at (315) 443-2515.

The Saltine Warrior was the admired mascot of the Syracuse University sports teams for many, many years. A male student was selected from one of the fraternities to wear the clothing of the Saltine Warrior—a brave man to lead the athletes to face their opponents. He was resplendent in his feathered war bonnet carrying the tomahawk to put fear in foes. The mascot was abolished by S.U. when Native Americans nationally objected to the use of symbols that were deemed derogatory. In a sense, they'll have some true Saltine Warriors attending classes.

I spoke with one of the Onondaga chiefs about The Promise and he advised me that 28 youths from the Onondaga Nation Territory will be attending Syracuse University in September of this year, 2007, not counting those Native Americans who hopefully will be admitted from neighboring communities as well as those already enrolled. This is more encouraging to see than just the few who earned scholarships in the past for excelling in a particular sport.

CHAPTER TWENTY-SIX

OTHER ISSUES

Before you pounce on me and tell me that the book is not complete, I'm letting you know that I have been advised by many not to explore or investigate the "Warrior Society." The following article quoted from *The Post-Standard* (source: *The Associated Press*) on Thursday, February 21, 2008 will give you some dynamics of the situation:

"New York—Three chiefs of the St. Regis Mohawks have filed a $60 million defamation lawsuit against the New York Post over editorials (that I've never read) blasting the Indian tribe as a criminal enterprise.

The Upstate tribe came under fire from the feisty tabloid over their proposal to build a $600 million casino in Monticello, 90 miles northwest of New York City in the Catskills.

The editorials, published Feb. 21, 2007, and Jan. 8, accuse the chiefs of 'serious crimes' and 'expose them to public contempt, ridicule, aversion and disgrace.'

The first editorial says the tribe was involved in a $687 million liquor, cigarette and gun smuggling ring, imported illegal immigrants from China and engaged in shootouts with police. The Jan. 8 editorial said the tribe 'amounts to a criminal enterprise.' Suzanne Halpin, a Post spokeswoman, said she had no comment on the lawsuit.

The lawsuit was filed Tuesday in Manhattan's state Supreme Court. It asks for $20 million in damages for each of the three chiefs, none of whom was mentioned in the editorials by name."

According to their web-site: www.sisis.nativeweb.org/mohawk/warrior2.html the *Rotiskenrakete*-Mohawk Warrior Society professes 4 principles—"*skennen, ioriwiio, kasastensera,* and *tekaiehnawakeon* which they say stands for peace, righteousness, strength, and unity. Therefore, violence and crime are not our way."

I don't have a law background so I don't want to present a side on casino issues (including Turning Stone); lands placed in Federal trust, or land rights issues. These are on-going issues and are the jurisdiction of the courts.

Another controversial issue is the tax-free sale of cigarettes. "The Onondaga sold more than 1 million cartons of cigarettes in 2005, the last year that complete records were available from the Department of Taxation and Finance. The Oneida Nation sold 2.1 million cartons. Figures for the other nations were unavailable." (*Post-Standard* Glenn Coin 2/1/07 pg. A-16)

On March 2, 2008, one year later, Mr. Coin reported the 2005 BIA (Bureau of Indian Affairs) figures at 1.2 million cartons of cigarettes*, 31 million gallons of gasoline, and sales of other products at $10.6 million.

* What happened to the missing 900,000 cartons?

"New York officials expect the state to receive at least $64.5 million in new revenues each year by taxing Native American sales of cigarettes and gasoline, but Onondaga Nation chiefs warn that the state could end up spending millions of dollars if the proposed tax ruins the economy on Indian territories.

The Seneca are also having trouble with New York State about the sales tax issue. They say that if New York persists, they will charge a $1.00 fee per car traveling in either direction on the New York State Thruway as it passes illegally* through their Cattaraugus Reservation near Irving, NY.

* www.wgrz.com/news/news_article.aspx?storyid=472913/4/2008

I personally join hundreds of motorists in line every Tuesday at the Canastota Oneida Nation Sav-On station to purchase my weekly supply of gasoline at a savings of anywhere from 13 to 21 cents per gallon. I bring extra, empty gas cans to add to what is put in the car—there is no limit. There is an extra savings if you pay by cash. The way prices are going on fuel, you might as well take advantage of this.

The Onondaga Nation's only regular source of income comes from tax-free cigarette sales. In recent years, the Onondaga have used their cigarette profits to build a $3 million project that brought drinking water to hundreds of nation residents whose wells were contaminated, and a $4 million lacrosse and hockey arena for the nation's youths.

Cigarette profits also pay for free substance abuse counseling for any Onondagan at the nation's rehabilitation center, fire protection services by the Onondaga Nation Fire Department, the salaries of the nation's security force and 65 workers at the Onondaga Nation Smoke Shop, and home repair grants for nation residents.

If the state insists on taxing the Onondaga Nation's cigarette sales to non-natives, the Onondaga Nation's shop will shut down, and the Onondaga people will become dependent on New York to pay for many basic services, Onondaga Chief Irving Powless said.

'All of the people working at our smoke shop will become unemployed,' Powless said. 'If they become unemployed, and go on welfare, how much will it cost the state?'

The Onondaga receive state money only for education and health services, Powless said."

The cigarette tax issue is perhaps more crucial to the Onondaga economy than to the economy at some other Indian territories in New York. The Onondaga chiefs and clan mothers oppose casino gambling. There is no casino at Onondaga. "We aren't going to have one," Powless said.

Meanwhile, the Oneida, Mohawk and Seneca nations own casinos, and the Cayuga are negotiating with the state to open one....

[Sid] Hill said the state's politicians who want to end the Onondaga Nation's tax-free business are the same leaders who willingly give other businesses millions of dollars in property tax breaks through the Empire Zone program."

(*Post-Standard* Mike McAndrew Nov. 18, 2003)

The latest edition of *Justice For Indigenous Peoples* came in the mail to me on Friday, July 18, 2008 so this will be an addendum to the copyright version of my book at the Library of Congress. It was printed by the Indian Law Resource Center in Helena, Montana.

Onondaga Land Rights Suit

"In 2005, the Onondaga Nation filed an historic lawsuit against the State of New York and others for stealing Nation lands in violation of federal [Federal] laws. The Onondaga case is an unusual lawsuit, remarkable because it seeks only a statement by the court that the land was illegally taken from the Nation and that the Nation continues to have legal title to the land. It does not ask for possession of the land nor for compensation. Driven primarily by its traditional responsibility to the Earth, the Nation is especially interested in securing clean-up of the many Superfund sites* in the area around Syracuse, especially Onondaga Lake.

The defendants asked that the suit be dismissed on the grounds that some 200 years have passed since the land was taken from the Nation and on the grounds that the State of New York is immune from suit.

In November 2006, we filed a massive and enormously important response to the motions to dismiss the Nation's suit. Supported by almost 900 pages of expert reports and historical materials prepared by our team of experts and researchers, our brief showed that the Nation did not delay, that the Nation continuously protested and sought to recover its lands, and that the passage of time has not resulted in any prejudice to the defendants.

In October 2007, the federal district court [Federal District Court] heard oral arguments in this case. We must now be patient as we await the court's decision. As we wait, we are encouraged by the Interior Department Solicitor's recommendation that the federal [Federal] government file supporting litigation against New York State."

Mohawk Land Claim

"After reaching an historic settlement agreement in the Mohawk land claim in early 2005, our efforts to bring some measure of justice to the Mohawk people for the land stolen from them over 200 years ago were set back by damaging court rulings made in other cases. These rulings influenced some of the local governments involved in the Mohawk claim to withdraw their support for the settlement. In response, we have pursued a dual approach to bring all the parties back to the settlement and to promote its implementation.

First, we have supported a public education and outreach campaign by the Mohawks to inform local communities about the many benefits of the settlement agreement, which would bring considerable financial gains to the non-Indian communities in the land claim area as well as increasing cooperation among Mohawk and non-Mohawk governments on such issues as environmental protection, land use, and building codes.

Second, we have pushed forward in court to show that our legal case remains strong despite the adverse rulings in other cases. In late 2006, the State of New York and other defendants in the case filed briefs asking the court to dismiss our case.

In response, we worked to show that this case should not be dismissed. The Mohawk case is unique because of the continued Mohawk presence in the claim area and because of federal [Federal] laws affecting Mohawk territory that do not apply elsewhere. Because the Mohawks have lived in and governed much of this area for many years—in some cases since the 19th century—we believe the case is fundamentally different from those filed by other Indian nations, most of whom were removed from their lands many years ago. In 2006, we hired a slate of experts in disciplines such as history, legal history, demography, statistics, and real estate appraisal to demonstrate the long-standing presence of the Mohawks in the claim area, the efforts made by the Mohawks to recover and protect their historic reservation lands, and the legal and practical barriers to those efforts. Our experts worked to produce reports, maps, title histories, and other documentation to support our briefs in the case, which were filed in mid-2007."

Tonawanda Seneca Nation Land Claim

"Like the Mohawks and the Onondagas, the Senecas were the victims of unlawful land deals with New York State that robbed them of much of their historic territory, including the Niagara River islands that were the subject of the land claim we filed on their behalf in 1933. Unfortunately, we have exhausted the legal avenues for restoring these lands. In the wake of this unjust result, we are working with the Nation to identify and pursue other initiatives to protect their rights to use and occupy their traditional lands."

Border-Crossing Rights

"In 2006, we launched an initiative to assist the Haudenosaunee (Six Nations Iroquois Confederacy) in protecting their rights to travel freely across the international border with Canada, a line that has falsely and arbitrarily divided Haudenosaunee communities since it was imposed upon them in the late 18th century. While this border-crossing right is protected by an international treaty, it has recently come under assault from misguided efforts by the federal [Federal] government to improve border security.

Together with the Tonawanda Seneca Nation and the Haudenosaunee, we are working to demonstrate to the United States government how the protection of Haudenosaunee treaty rights and recognition of Haudenosaunee sovereignty will enhance, not harm, border security.

*A Superfund site is an uncontrolled or abandoned place where hazardous waste is located, possibly affecting local ecosystems or people. Sites are listed on the National Priorities List (NPL) upon completion of the Hazard Ranking System (HRS) screening, public solicitation of comments about the proposed site, and after all comments have been addressed. (www.epa.gov/superfund/sites/index.htm7/21/2008)

I wrote earlier in the book about the dramatic drop in population of the Native Americans but I'm pleased to show to you the figures released in 1995 on the population up-surge:

The Cherokee Nation still remains the largest at 369,035. The Iroquois Confederacy (ranked #8) has grown from 38,218 to 52,557 in 2000. Total Native American population figures enjoy a dramatic increase from 1.8 million in 1990 to 2.48 million identifying themselves as Native American in 2000, a 10 year span! This is most encouraging.

Getting back to the start of the book; those in attendance on March 11, 2005 about the land rights were the Federal government clerk situated behind bullet-proof glass,

Robert T. Coulter (Tim)
    Attorney-At-Law, Executive Director Indian Law Resource Center
Debra Reed   Development Director   "   "   "
Brooke Swaney Pepion   Assoc.   "   "   "   "
Joseph J. Heath, Attorney-At-Law, general counsel for the Onondaga Nation
Dorothy Webster, Eel Clan Mother-Onondaga Nation
Oren Lyons, Faith Keeper-Onondaga Nation
Chief Jake Edwards-Onondaga Nation
Chief Sid Hill, (Onondaga)-*Tadodaho* of the Haudenosaunee

—and me!

At the Federal Building, legal papers were submitted in triplicate or more, and were passed through a hole in a bullet-proof glass window encasing the Federal clerk (due, I suppose, to 911). After the legalities, I permanently "borrowed" the clerk's .89 cent **Bic** pen which was used for the signing. It became a gift to Sid later in the day. A luncheon was held in the Onondaga longhouse kitchen for the press, lawyers, out-of-town visitors, politicians, residents, chiefs, and clan mothers.

My presentation to him included the words, "They stole your land, I stole their pen." This brought some laughter particularly from a reporter who claimed to be from the *New York Times*.

**These next three articles will be an addenda to my original manuscript sent to the Library of Congress for copyright purposes. These addenda are dated August 22, 2008, June 4, 2008 and August 21, 2008. References are added to my bibliography for your edification.

I came across an article that Canterbury Tours and Services at 51 Comstock Rd. in Tunkhannock, PA are conducting a tour of the historical sites of the Haudenosaunee Holocaust. I'll briefly tell you about it but you'll gain more information by contacting them directly at www.canterburyts.com or 1-877-664-4714 (toll free).

"This narrated trip travels the route of the Revolutionary War campaign known commonly as Sullivan's March. Although there is debate among scholars as to whether Sullivan was ultimately considered 'successful' in his military mission, there is no doubt that the events of May through September, 1779 were both an astounding military feat and a tragic devastation of ancient Native communities.

Hear amazing real stories of the complex political causes and far-reaching cultural consequences of Sullivan's March. Follow ancient Native paths through breathtaking scenery from Easton, PA to Elmira, NY. It was along this route that General Sullivan led his army on the first leg of the 1779 military march against the Haudenosaunee people—known to the English as 'The Six Nations' and to the French as 'The Iroquois Confederacy'. This is an unforgettable story that's largely forgotten in our modern day. It must be re-told.

As you ride, your guide will continue [to] unfold the incredible story of the tumultuous political events leading up to the March, recorded victoriously by American historians, but remembered much differently by those of Native descent. (Canterbury Tours)

INDIAN COUNTRY TODAY June 4, 2008 "SYRACUSE, N.Y. - On April 17, [2008] students at Syracuse University were told about a little-known part of New York State history. In 1779, under the direction of George Washington, armies of men stormed central New York, burning villages and crops and sending Iroquois people – particularly the Cayuga – away from their homelands.

The genocide, known as the *1779 Sullivan-Clinton Campaign*, was captured in journal and letter writing by Washington, who ordered Major General John Sullivan and Major General James Clinton to see to the 'total destruction and devastation' of Indian villages.

It was a political move on Washington's part; but more than two centuries later, the aftermath of that genocide continues to haunt the Cayuga. To this day, they are living hundreds of miles away from their homeland; others eventually settled in Oklahoma, others at the Six Nations territory in Ontario [Canada].

'They fled west, they fled north, some went south,' said Brooke Hansen, of Ithaca College's anthropology department.

In 2001, a group of activists and professors, including Hansen, came together to discuss ways in which they could educate non-Natives in New York about the Cayuga, and also possibly help the Cayuga come back to their homeland. The *Strengthening Haudenosaunee American Relations Through Education* group was formed as a result, and they continue to educate and promote awareness today.

On April 17, Hansen and a colleague at Ithaca College, Jack Rossen, spoke to Syracuse University students about the SHARE program and the Cayuga.

'We're trying to educate the broader non-Native community,' Hansen said. 'We go into every single school in our district here and we talk to you [students] about the history of Native people right here in our area.'

'One of the things that we're always surprised about is these kids have never heard of the Sullivan Campaign. It was one of the most significant events of genocide in our area.'

Through presentations, Hansen and her SHARE colleagues try to spread education of Indian history and presence.

Speaking with adult-aged students at SU, Hansen and Rossen broadened their scope of education, speaking partly about the SHARE program and what they have accomplished, but also exploring the entire anti-Indian movement and why individuals might join such a cause.

'It's usually just a lack of education,' Hansen said. 'We talked about those broader issues that really brought SHARE to light.'

SHARE's single most celebrated accomplishment was its assistance in bringing an old farm back to the possession of the Cayuga. In 2001, when SHARE was formed, the Cayuga had no property in their original homelands. Part of SHARE's goal was to change that. 'We started by just doing education and then the opportunity arose to buy this farm,' Hansen said. 'We thought that's exactly what we wanted to accomplish.'

The farm was purchased and by 2005, the Cayuga were ready to completely take it over. It has been in their possession ever since. 'It was the first single piece of property they got back in their homeland,' Hansen said. The farm is located in Springport, about 30 miles north of Ithaca. The land has an old house on site and when the Cayuga took over ownership, Dan Hill volunteered to take on the task of running the farm. 'He was the first Cayuga to move back to the homeland in 200 years,' Hansen said.

Fittingly, the Cayuga SHARE farm is where the center of the Cayuga Nation used to be. The area was once home to more than 50 longhouses. 'We were really lucky that the 70 acre farm we were able to acquire was really smack-dab in the middle of the Cayuga ancestral homelands,' Hansen said. The farm currently has a 70-tree apple orchard with different types of apples, a medicinal herb garden, berry patches, and a big old, beautiful farm house.

Members of SHARE and the Cayuga from all over visit the farm regularly to help Hill keep it maintained. With a service-list keeping volunteers in contact, Hill is able to call for a 'work day' and dozens of students, volunteers, and Cayuga will travel to the farm for the day and do whatever work needs to be done. The farm is also used for many education events and there are plans to construct a longhouse there to begin the process of re-teaching Cayuga culture.

The long-term goal is to eventually have several Cayuga families move to the farm and start a community. The shorter-term goal is to bring more Cayuga to the farm on a regular basis to let them get their hands dirty in their ancestral land.

Two-hundred years after being driven away, the Cayuga now have the opportunity to go back." (Shannon Burns *Indian Country Today*)

"Clint Halftown and Tim Twoguns looked out on the long tasseled rows of Iroquois white corn and the low-lying bean and squash plants (the three sisters) in a field off Route 414 just inside the village of Seneca Falls.

They smiled because they liked what they saw on this cloud-covered

Tuesday morning and what they foresee as sunny days ahead for their garden and for their tribe, the Cayuga Indian Nation of New York.

Both men were also keenly aware that history was playing out before them sure as the corn, beans and squash were ready to be picked.

The significance? It's the first time the Cayuga have planted and reaped food from their Finger Lakes homeland since their ancestors fled the region more than 200 years ago.

'This is very important to our people because this is the land we should have been upon. This land is ours,' said Halftown, the Cayuga's federally recognized spokesman. He and Twoguns were in town to help pack boxes of fresh vegetables—including cucumbers, sweet corn and zucchini—that were harvested from the garden. The produce was to be delivered today to about 90 tribal member households living in the Greater Buffalo area. The food is free to them.

The garden, named 'Gakwiyo' which is Cayuga for 'good food', also symbolizes the nation's efforts to re-sink roots in their native homeland. Some day, Twoguns said, he hopes to see other Cayuga living in the area, working the ground.

The nation hired Bill Turnbull, a long-time Geneva-area farmer, to run their fledgling farming operations. He put in a 25-acre garden and a huge swath of soy beans in a 100-acre field that the nation acquired in April.

The Cayuga also built a large pole barn on the property to store their harvest and farming equipment. The nation is also canning vegetables for its members and plans to plant more berries, fruit trees and vegetables in the near future.

In recent years, the Cayuga have purchased several businesses, a mansion and hundreds of acres in their ancestral homeland in Cayuga and Seneca counties. They're still trying to gain sovereign tax-free use of their holdings through the federal [Federal] trust process but have met stiff opposition from both counties and the state. They want the Cayuga to pay their fair share of taxes and to follow local laws. The dispute remains unsettled.

Twoguns said he got the idea for the garden after reading about groups of people who only eat food produced within 100 miles of where they live.

'I thought this would be great for our people and that wouldn't it be great to be doing what our ancestors used to do in their day,' he said.

Corn, beans and squash hold symbolic importance for the Cayuga.

They call them the 'three sisters' and they're part of the Nation's creation story, symbolizing 'Mother Earth sustaining us,' Twoguns said.

He and Halftown see a bright future for the remaining 500 or so Cayuga, most of whom live in Western New York or out of state. A future that involves the Cayuga strengthening ties to their homeland by buying and developing more property around the north end of Cayuga Lake.

'We're not going away. We've got one foot in the door and we're going to kick it wide open,' Halftown said. (Scott Rapp *The Post-Standard* August 20, 2008)

Voices

"We believe in our hearts that we are the environment. Just like the plants, the animals…We've got a lot of work to do. We can't do it ourselves…We've got to all work together on this."

Onondaga Chief Jake Edwards

"In some ways, it [filing the Onondaga Land Rights Action] feels like a culmination of all these generations of people. I have seen tears for the elders…Some of them would say, 'I wonder if this will ever happen?'"

Audrey Shenandoah

"The women of our community have decided that it is time to act. It is time to clean up our mother [Earth]."

Onondaga Chief Bradley Powless

"We know what it's like to lose our land…Displacement is something we wouldn't want to put on anyone because our ancestors have suffered from it."

Onondaga *Tadadaho* Sid Hill

"There is plenty of land for everyone…What defines us is how we acquired it and how we take care of it."

Jack Edgerton-author

Neighbors and acquaintances of mine use the same expressions today as they previously did when I told them of my writings on the European Holocaust—"Why would I want to go there? Why do you bother to show interest in them? Do you think that you're going to change anything?" If by my being "active" in educating others about some of the injustices in the world makes me an "activist," then so be it.

CHANGE IS GOOD—YOU GO FIRST!

I hope to educate the "*ants*" of the world i.e. the *ignorants* and the *arrogants*.

BIBLIOGRAPHY

LIBRARY SOURCES:

Alfred, Taiaiake Peace Power Righteousness—an indigenous manifesto Oxford University Press 1999

Alfred, Taiaiake *Wasase*—indigenous pathways of action Broadview Press 2005

Allen, James Paul and Turner, Eugene James We The People MacMillan Pub. 1988

Anguish, Lena Putnam History of Fayetteville-Manlius Area Fayetteville-Manlius School District 1966

Arden, Harvey The Fire That Never Dies National Geographic Society September 1987

Beauchamp, William M. A History of the New York Iroquois Ira J. Friedman 1968

Beauchamp, William Martin The Iroquois Trail Beauchamp Recorder Office 1892

Bernardi, Roy A. Syracuse-Center of an Empire Towery Publishing 1998

Billard, Jules B. We Americans National Geographic Society 1975

Bradfield, Gerald E. Fort William Henry-Digging up History The French and Indian War Society 2001

Bruchac, Joseph Indian Renaissance National Geographic Society September 2004

Burenhult, Dr. Goran Traditional Peoples Today Weldon Owen Pty Ltd/ Bra Bocker AB 1994

Clark, Joshua Onondaga; Reminiscences of Earlier and Later Times Vol. 1 Syracuse, Stoddard, and Babcock 1849

Clayton, W.W. History of Onondaga County (1615-1878) D. Mason & Co. 1878

Condon, George E. Stars in the Water-the story of the Erie Canal Doubleday & Co. 1974

Cooper, Michael L. Indian School—Teaching the White Man's Way Clarion Books 1999

Davis, Christopher North American Indian Hamlyn Publishing Group Ltd. 1969

Fisher, Donald M. Lacrosse-A History of the Game The Johns Hopkins University Press 2002

Gottesman, Ronald Violence in America Charles Scribner's Sons 1999

Graymont, Barbara The Iroquois in the American Revolution Syracuse University Press 1972

Hirschfelder, Arlene Native Americans Dorling Kindersley Publishing 2000

Hodge, Frederick Webb Handbook of American Indians Pageant Books, Inc. 1960

Jenkinson, Clay Straus Message on the Wind The Marmarth Press 2002

Josephy, Alvin M. The American Heritage Book of Indians American Heritage Publishing Company 1961

LaFarge, Oliver A Pictorial History of the American Indian Crown Publishing 1956

Lopez, Barry H. The Rediscovery of North America The University Press of Kentucky 1990

Mann, Barbara Alice George Washington's War on Native America 2005 (special loan from Hunter College Library-New York City)

McCarthy, Richard L. and Newman, H. The Iroquois Vol. IV 1960

Morgan, Lewis Henry League of the Iroquois Corinth Books 1962

Nabokov, Peter. Native American Testimony Penguin Group 1978

National Geographic The New Face of the American Indian—Scenes From a Renaissance September 2004

National Geographic From One Sovereign People to Another September 1987

Nerburn, Kent. The Wisdom of the Native Americans New World Library 1999

Norbeck, Oscar E. Book of Authentic Indian Life Crafts Galloway Corp.1974

Parfit, Michael Hunt for the First Americans National Geographic Society 2000

Richards, Frank E. Richards Atlas of New York State Frank E. Richards 1967

Ritchie, William A. The Archeology of New York State National History Press 1965

Sale, Kirkpatrick The Conquest of Paradise Alfred A Knopf Pub. 1990

Schramm, Henry W. Central New York Donning Co. Pub. 1989

Sforza-Cavalli, Luigi Luca and Francesco Cavalli-Sforza The Great Human Diasporas (special loan from New York State Library-Albany) Addison-Wesley Publishing Company 1993

Shreeve, James The Greatest Journey-National Geographic March 2006

Taylor, Colin F. The Native Americans-The Indigenous People of North America Salamander Books, Ltd. 2002

Tuck, James A. Onondaga Iroquois Prehistory Syracuse University Press 1971

Webb, Stephen Saunders 1676-The End of American Independence Alfred A. Knopf Pub. 1984

Wilbur, C. Keith M.D. The Woodland Indians The Globe Pequot Press 1995

Williams, Ted. The Reservation Syracuse University Press 1976

Zona, Guy A. The Soul Would Have No Rainbow If the Eyes Had No Tears Simon & Schuster 1994

INTERNET SOURCES:

www.iroquoismuseum.org/3/21/05
www.home.hetnet.nl/~fatcat/military.html
www.college.hmco.com/history/readerscomp/naind/html/na_014200_handsomelake.htm
www.philtar.ucsm.ac.uk/encyclopedia/nam/handsome.html
www.pbs.org/thewarthatmadeamerica/timeline.html11/26/2006
www.recordonline.com/archive/2005/02/15/oneidas.htm
www.sunysb.edu/libmap/img0017b.jpg
www.turtleislandchautauqua.org/holocaust.html11/21/2005

www.shelbycountyhistory.org/schs/indians/amerinds.htm3/21/2006

www.historicaltextarchive.com/sections.php?op=viewarticle&artid=
7503/21/2006

www.white-history.com/hwr50.htm3/30/2006

www.symposium.syr.edu

www.law.syr.edu/academics/centers/ilgc/research%20papers.asp?css=
11/20/2006

www.law.syr.edu/academics/centers/ilgc/Haudenosaunee%202%20
draft%20agend...

www.law.syr.edu/indigenous(CILGC Working Paper No. 05-1)

www.indiancountry.com/content.cfm?id=108428527110/24/2005

www.iroquoismuseum.org/corn.htm4/2/2006

www.plaza.ufl.edu/ashley/index.htm

www.asylumnation.com/asylum/_r/showthread/threadid_27741/index.html

www.mnsu.edu/emuseum/information/biography/klmno/morgan_lewis_
henry.html10/14/2005

www.en.wikipedia.org/wiki/Louis_Henry_Morgan10/14/2005

www.absoluteastronomy.com/encyclopedia/i/ir/iroquois_kinship.
htm10/14/2005

www.canadiana.org/citm/themes/aboriginals/aboriginals4_e.html9/
26/2005

www.u-s-history.com/pages/h1214.html9/26/2005

www.reference.com/browse/wiki/Treaty_of_Fort_Stanwix9/26/2005

www.u-s-history.com/pages/h1215.html9/26/2005

www.college.hmco.com/history/readerscomp/naind/html/
na_040200_treatiesoffo.htm9/26/2005

www.sni.org/treaty.html9/26/2005

www.ganondagan.org/treaty.html9/26/2005

www.degiyagoh.net/guswenta_two_row.htm10/25/2005

www.degiyagoh.net/book_canandaigua_treaty.htm9/26/2005

www.oneida-nation.net/TREATY-KO.html9/26/2005

www.ratical.org/many_worlds/6Nations/TreatyRights.html9/26/2005

www.nytimes.com/books/01/01/07/reviews/010107.07anderst.
html9/26/2005

www.canandaigua-treaty.org/canandaigua_treaty_commemoration.
html11/8/2005

www.canandaigua-treaty.org/Why the need for a Treaty 1. html11/9/2005

www.canandaigua-treaty.org/The Canandaigua Treaty of 1794. html11/9/2005

www.canandaigua-treaty.org/Treaty Committee Index.html10/25/2005

www.pbs.org/weta/thewest/resources/archives/eight/dawes.htm9/15/2005

www.dickshovel.com/cleansing.html9/15/2005

www.search.msn.com/previewx.aspx?q=Indian+Appropriation+ Act&FORM=CBPW&fir...2005

www.marketplacesolutions.net/secure/heritagebooks/merchant2/ merchant.mvc?Screen=P...10/11/2005

www.rootsweb.com/~srgp/articles/sullcamp.htm2006

www.rootsweb.com/~nyononda/ONONDAGA/HISTORY.HTM2006

www.care.diabetesjournals.org/cgi/content/abstract/23/12/17862006

www.laplaza.org/health/dwc/nadp/eaglestory.html4/4/2006

www.diabetes.org/communityprograms-and-localevents/nativeamericans. jsp4/4/2006

www.diabetes.org/type-1-diabetes.jsp4/4/2006

www.diabetes.org/type-2-diabetes.jsp4/4/2006

www.diabetes.org/weightloss-and-exercise/weightloss.jsp4/4/2006

www.care.diabetesjournals.org/cgi/content/abstract/23/12/1786

www.montana.edu/wwwai/imsd/diabetes/serious.htm4/4/2006

www.pbs.org/thewarthatmadeamerica/timeline.html2006

www.carnegiemuseums.org/cmnh/exhibits/north-south-east-west/ iroquois/three_sister...4/5/2006

www.landscaping.about.com/cs/soilfertilizers/a/companion_plant. htm4/5/2006

www.bioneers.org/programs/food_farming/iwc.php4/5/2006

www.redhawkslax.com/news.lacrossemag.html4/1/2006

www.wheretheyplaygames.com/People.asp4/1/2006

www.philtar.ucsm.ac.uk/encyclopedia/nam/handsome.html3/9/2006

www.college.hmco.com/history/readerscomp/naind/html/ na_014200_handsomelake.htm3/9/2006

www.recordonline.com/archive/2005/02/15/oneidas1.htm10/25/2005

www.home.hetnet.nl/~fatcat/military.html9/25/2005

www.indianlaw.org/2005

www.indianlaw.org/onondaga.html7/2/2005

www.turtleislandchautauqua.org/holocaust.html2005

www.digital.library.upenn.edu/women/marshall/country/country-IV-36.
html7/12/2006

www.en.wikipedia.org/wiki/Dutch_Empire7/12/2006

www.lacrosse-network.com/outsidersguide/history.htm7/19/2006

www.syracusehalloffame.com/pages/inductees/2004/gordy_ohstrom.
html7/19/2006

www.come2az.com/azsports/deserthockey.htm7/19/2006

www.syracuse.com/news/indianlandclaims/poststandard/index.ssf?/news/
indianland7/19/2006

www.youthlacrosseusa.com/generalnews/111803_NTtaxonNative
Amcigsales.html7/19/2006

www.gerflortaraflex.com/press/Taraflex_at_Onondaga.htm7/19/2006

www.brneurosci.org/smallpox.html7/19/2006

www.tafkac.org/medical/smallpox/smallpox_blankets.html7/19/2006

www.bbc.co.uk/history/war/coldwar/pox_weapon_01.shtml7/19/2006

www.nativeweb.org/pages/legal/amherst/lord_jeff.html7/19/2006

www.onondaganation.org/media.today.html7/19/2006

www.onondaganation.org/media.facts.html7/19/2006

www.onondaganation.org/media.environment.html7/19/2006

www.onondaganation.org/media.sovereignty.html7/19/2006

www.onondaganation.org/media.today.html7/19/2006

www.redhawkslax.com/news.lacrossemag.html7/19/2006

www.redhawkslax.com/arena.html7/19/2006

www.onondaganation.org/history.timeline.html7/19/2006

www.onondaganation.org/history.html7/19/2006

www.onondaganation.org/history.quotes.html7/19/2006

www.choice101.com/19-lies.html7/26/2006

www.cowboysindians.com/articles/archives/0999/karl_may.html7/
26/2006

www.mynewsletterbuilder.com/tools/view_newsletter.php?newsletter_
id=14095575058/3/2006

www.easterndoor.com/archives/VOL.7/7-05.htm8/3/2006

www.tuscaroras.com/jtlc/The_Great_Law/chief_jake_thomas_
clanmothers_role_pg18/3/2006

www.championtrees.org/peace/PrayersforPeace04.htm8/3/2006
www.championtrees.org/yarrow/Treeof Peace.htm8/3/2006
www.peacecouncil.net/noon8/3/2006
www.hometown.aol.com/miketben/miketben.htm8/2/2006
www.etext.virginia.edu/etcbin/toccer-new2?id=WasFi12.xml&images=
    images/modeng&d6/19/2006
www.army.mil/cmh-pg/documents/RevWar/revra.htm8/31/2006
www.en.wikipedia.org/wiki/Solvay_process1/11/2007
www.oldandsold.com/canada/kingston-3.shtml1/16/2007
www.usahistory.com/wars/william.htm1/16/2007
www.san.beck.org/11-6-NewFrance1663-1744.html1/16/2007
www.wvculture.org/history/indland.html1/22/2007
www.agt.net/public/dgarneau/indian13.htm1/18/2007
www.home.ptd.net/~nikki/indian.htm6/13/2007
www.yale.edu/lawweb/avalon/ntreaty/six1794.htm6/13/2007
www.yale.edu/lawweb/avalon/ntreaty/six1789.htm6/13/2007
www.enterprisecommunity.org/programs/native_american/6/13/2007
www.ifapray.org/NativeAmericanPrayer/NAPA00/NAPA_2_7_00.
    html6/13/2007
www.hud.gov/offices/pih/ih/homeownership/184/6/13/2007
www.en.wikipedia.org/wiki/Joseph_Brant7/18/2007
www.letchworthparkhistory.com/treaties.html7/16/2007
www.kahonwes.com/time/1700.htm7/16/2007
www.onondaganation.org/treaties.stanwix.html7/16/2007
www.onondaganation.org/treaties.html7/16/2007
www.nps.gov/fost/7/16/2007
www.ohiohistorycentral.org/entry.php?rec=20757/16/2007
www.en.wikipedia.org/wiki/Royal_Proclamation_of_17637/16/2007
www.championtrees.org/Dragon/chptr11.htm6/18/2007
www.yale.edu/lawweb/avalon/ntreaty/six1789.htm6/13/2007
www.yale.edu/lawweb/avalon/ntreaty/six1794.htm6/13/2007
www.home.ptd.net/~nikki/indian.htm6/13/2007
www.enterprisecommunity.org/programs/native_american/6/13/2007
www.ifapray.org/NativeAmericanPrayer/NAPAOO/NAPA_2_7_00.
    html6/13/2007
www.hud.gov/offices/pih/ih/homeownership/184/6/13/2007

www.hud.gov/utilities/print/print2.cfm?page=80$^@http%3A%2F%2Fwww%2Ehu...6/13/2007

www.en.wikipedia.org/wiki/Wyoming_Valley_battle_and_massacre7/2/2007

www.jmu.edu/madison/center/main_pages/madison_archives/era/native/iroquois/bkgr...7/2/2007

www.army.mil/cmh-pg/reference/revbib/westo.htm7/2/2007

www.pequotmuseum.org/NativeLifeways/Clothing/7/13/2007

www.pequotmuseum.org/NativeLifeways/Transportation/7/13/2007

www.pequotmuseum.org/NativeLifeways/FishingToolsTechniques/7/13/2007

www.pequotmuseum.org/NativeLifeways/HuntingToolsTechniques/7/13/2007

www.pequotmuseum.org/NativeLifeways/EarlyAgriculture/7/13/2007

www.pequotmuseum.org/NativeLifeways/HarvestingMaize/7/13/2007

www.pequotmuseum.org/NativeLifeways/MakingaMeal/7/13/2007

www.pequotmuseum.org/NativeLifeways/MakingCeramics/7/13/2007

www.pequotmuseum.org/SocietyCulture/AncientHuntingCommunities/7/13/2007

www.pequotmuseum.org/SocietyCulture/AFamilyGroupca1500/7/13/2007

www.pequotmuseum.org/SocityCulture/TheEarlyFurTrade/7/13/2007

www.pequotmuseum.org/SocietyCulture/WhytheEuropeansCame/7/13/2007

www.pequotmuseum.org/SocietyCulture/TheImpactofDisease/7/13/2007

www.pequotmuseum.org/SocietyCulture/LandLossBegins/7/13/2007

www.pequotmuseum.org/SocietyCulture/NativesandChristianity/7/13/2007

www.pequotmuseum.org/SocietyCulture/HoldontotheLand/7/13/2007

www.pequotmuseum.org/SocietyCulture/ANewGenerationofLeaders/7/13/2007

www.pequotmuseum.org/TheNaturalWorld/GlaciersandtheLand/7/13/2007

www.pequotmuseum.org/TheNaturalWorld/EarlyMammalsoftheNortheast/7/13/2007

www.pequotmuseum.org/TheNaturalWorld/1714000YearsAgo/7/13/2007

www.pequotmuseum.org/TheNaturalWorld/1412000YearsAgo/7/13/2007
www.pequotmuseum.org/TheNaturalWorld/1210000YearsAgo/
7/13/2007
www.pequotmuseum.org/TheNaturalWorld/108000YearsAgo/7/13/2007
www.pequotmuseum.org/TheNaturalWorld/84000YearsAgo/7/13/2007
www.pequotmuseum.org/TheNaturalWorld/4000350YearsAgo/
7/13/2007
www.pequotmuseum.org/TheNaturalWorld/350YearsAgoPresent/
7/13/2007
www.pequotmuseum.org/NativeLifeways/BuildingaWigwam/7/13/2007
www.careers3.accenture.com/Careers/Canada/NewGraduates/
Aboriginal Internships/Abor...7/13/2007
www.home.epix.net/~landis/histry.html7/13/2007
www.pequotmuseum.org/TribalHistory/TribalHistoryOverview/
MashantucketPequot...7/13/2007
www.members.aol.com/Nowacumig/biograph.html7/13/2007
www.wvculture.org/history/indland.html7/13/2007
www.en.wikipedia.org/wiki/Wyoming Valley7/13/2007
www.en.wikipedia.org/wiki/Albany Congress7/13/2007
www.virginiaplaces.org/settleland/treaties.html7/13/2007
www.libr.unl.edu:8888/etext/treaties/treaty.00005.html7/13/2007
www.whitehouse.gov/history/presidents/gwl.html7/12/2007
www.iroquoisnationals.com/program.html7/12/2007
www.redhawkslax.com/srhome.html7/12/2007
www.earthheart.com/NativeMedicine&Readings.htm5/25/2007
www.nativetech.org/plants/sweetgrass.html5/25/2007
www.en.wikipedia.org/wiki/Tobacco5/25/2007
www.answers.com/topic/native-american5/25/2007
www.en.wikipedia.org/wiki/Sullivan Expedition5/24/2007
www.en.wikipedia.org/wiki/Cherry Valley Massacre5/24/2007
www.answers.com/topic/iroquois4/25/20074/25/2007
www.cowboysindians.com/articles/archives/0999/karl may.
html7/26/2006
www.sixnations.buffnet.net/Lessons from History/8/9/2006
www.tuscaroras.com/jtlc/The Great Law/chief jake thomas
clanmothers role pg1....8/3/2006

www.lamokawaneta.com/LamokaLake.html3/30/2005

www.religioustolerance.org/ce.htm11/2/2005

www.garynull.com/Documents/nativeamerican.htm5/25/2007

www.peacecouncil.net/noon2007

www.onondaganation.org/landclaims.html9/11/2006

www.peace4turtleisland.org/pages/onondagapressrelease.htm9/11/2006

www.iaiachronicle.org/archives/Onondagafrazier2005.htm9/11/2006

www.championtrees.org/yarrow/landclaim.htm9/11/2006

www.indianlaw.org/onondaga.html9/11/2006

www.syracuse.com/news/indianlandclaims/poststandard/index.ssf?/news/
    indianland...7/19/2006

www.youthlacrosseusa.com/generalnews/111803_NTtaxonNative
    Amcigsales.html7/19/2006

www.gerflortaraflex.com/press/Taraflex_at_Onondaga.htm7/19/2006

www.come2az.com/azsports/deserthockey.htm7/19/2006

www.redhawkslax.com/news.lacrossemag.html7/19/2006

www.onondaganation.org/history.quotes.html7/19/2006

www.lacrosse-network.com/outsidersguide/history.htm7/19/2006

www.syracusehalloffame.com/pages/inductees/2004/gordy_ohstrom.
    html7/19/2006

www.sixnations.buffnet.net/Threats_to_Traditional_Governments/
    8/9/2006

www.indianlandtenure.org/ILTFallotment/histlegis/General
    AllotmentAct.htm3/21/2007

www.en.wikipedia.org/wiki/Solvay_process1/11/2007

www.rootsweb.com/~nyononda/CLARK.HTM7/28/2006

www.en.wikipedia.org/wiki/Sullivan_Expedition6/19/2006

www.sullivanclinton.com/6/19/2006

www.etext.virginia.edu/etcbin/toccer-new2?id=WasFil2.xml&images/
    modeng&d...6/19/2006

www.en.wikipedia.org/wiki/American_Revolutionary_War8/1/2006

www.tafkac.org/medical/smallpox/smallpox_blankets.html7/19/2006

www.brneurosci.org/smallpox.html7/19/2006

www.bbc.co.uk/history/war/coldwar/pox_weapon_01.shtml7/19/2006

www.nativeweb.org/pages/legal/amherst/lord_jeff.html7/19/2006

www.johnstown.com/johnson.html7/28/2006

www.earlyamerica.com/review/fall96/johnson.html8/24/2006
www.oldandsold.com/canada/kingston-3.shtml1/16/2007
www.usahistory.com/wars/william.htm1/16/20071/16/2007
www.usgennet.org/usa/ny/state/his/bk11/chl/pt4.html7/28/2006
www.army.mil/cmh-pg/documents/RevWar/revra.htm8/31/2006
www.san.beck.org/11-6-NewFrance1663-1744.html1/16/2007
www.blupete.com/Hist/BiosNS/1700-63/Subercase.htm1/16/2007
www.agt.net/public/dgarneau/indian13.htm1/18/2007
www.en.wikipedia.org/wiki/Dutch_Empire7/12/2006
www.digital.library.upenn.edu/women/marshall/country/country-IV-36.
    html7/12/2006
www.coins.nd.edu/ColCoin/ColCoinIntros/NNHistory.html7/12/2006
www.en.wikipedia.org/wiki/Manhattan7/24/20067/24/2006
www.rootsweb.com/%7Enyononda/SOLDLOTS.HTM5/18/2006
www.rootsweb.com/%7Enyononda/MANLIUS/REVWARSO.
    HTM5/18/2006
www.rootsweb.com/~nyononda/ONONDAGA/HISTORY.HTM1/
    22/2006
www.rootsweb.com/~srgp/articles/sullcamp.htm1/4/2006
www.bettinger.org/pages/775124/page775124.html?refresh=108234
    840429612/13/2005
www.tolatsga.org/iro.html4/7/2006
www.collegefund.org/about/history.html7/24/2007
www.hometown.aol.com/miketben/miketben.htm10/18/2004
www.syracuseprogressive.blogspot.com/2005/03/onondaga-nation-files-
    historic-land.html12/1/2005
www.tuscaroras.com/graydeer/pages/lawstory.htm12/1/2005
www.hayehwatha.org/1htpages/history.html12/1/2005
www.h2oman.blogspot.com/2005/01/tadodaho-leon-shenandoah.
    html12/1/2005
www.peace4turtleisland.org/pages/tributetoshenandoah.htm12/1/2005
www.nahm.org/AboutUs.html11/28/2005 (Native American Holocaust
    Museum)
www.onondaganationschool.org8/8/2007
www.lafayetteschools.org8/8/2007
www.redhawkslax.com/news.sacredsport.html2/10/2008

www.nll.com/careerstats.php2/18/2008
www.en.wikipedia.org/wiki/Vikings2/24/2008
www.dnaancestryproject.com/ydna_ancestry.php2/21/2008
www.simonpure.com/schemitzun_print.htm2/21/2008
www.midtel.net/~iroquois/ceremonies.htm2/7/2008
www.pulse.igc.org/archive/Aug00/2220.html2/7/2008
www.epa.gov/superfund/sites/index.htm7/21/2008
www.epa.gov/region02/superfund/7/21/2008
www.indiancountry.com/content.cfm?id=10964174248/21/2008

NEWSPAPER and TELEVISION:

Syracuse Herald-Journal Marcus Hayes Sacred Sport April 9, 1992

Post-Standard "Lacrosse Lessons Last Lifetime" Dick Case May 8, 2003

Post-Standard "Indian Casinos See Rapid Growth" Erica Werner February 16, 2005

TWEAN News Channel of Syracuse, LLC, d/b/a News 10 Now "Onondaga Nation makes land claim" Jim Lokay March 11, 2005

Post-Standard "For *tadodaho*, sorrow accompanies land claim" Sean Kirst March 11, 2005

The New York Times "Tribe Lays Claim…." Kirk Semple March 12, 2005

Post-Standard "First, Acid Rain; Now, Mercury" editorial March 14, 2005

Post-Standard "State Urged to Drop Immunity" John O'Brien March 16, 2005

Post-Standard "Tribal rivalry no factor…." Mike McAndrew March 21, 2005

Post-Standard "No matter how it's used, land still is Indian's" Angelica Wolfe October 7, 2005

Post-Standard "Ogdensburg group fights for fort" William Kates October 9, 2005

Post-Standard "No Telling" Peter Lyman October 11, 2005

Post-Standard "Lake Half-Clean? Not So Fast" Oren Lyons October 17, 2005

Post-Standard "Repeating History?" Doug George-Kanentiio October 24, 2005

Post-Standard "Can land be sovereign and taxable at the same time?" editorial November 1, 2005

Post-Standard "Famous New Yorkers IV—Cornplanter" Vicki Krisak November 2, 2005

Post-Standard "Ceremony Recalls 1794 Treaty" Sarah Moses November 12, 2005

Post-Standard "Tribes see threats..." Glenn Coin November 20, 2005

Empire Monthly "Conventions become...." Donna Reynolds December 2005

Post-Standard "Buried mercury...." Mark Weiner December 4, 2005

Post-Standard "CNY defies national trend" Marnie Eisenstadt December 14, 2005

PBS—WQED "The War That Made America" January 18 and 25, 2006

Post-Standard "Sovereignty is owed to Onondagas despite courts" September 1, 2006

Post-Standard "Historic Pact To Clean Lake" Mark Weiner and Delen Goldberg October 12, 2006

Post-Standard "Doubts remain..." Sean Kirst October 13, 2006

Post-Standard "How To Detoxify Onondaga Lake" Delen Goldberg October 15, 2006

Post-Standard "ESF launches Native Peoples Center" Delen Goldberg October 18, 2006

Post-Standard "Why did Onondagas dig through old records?" Tony Burnett November 30, 2006

Post-Standard "Helping A Craft Stick It Out" Alaina Potrikus December 3, 2006

Post-Standard "Onondaga Plan To Roll Their Own Cigarettes" Mike McAndrew December 13, 2006

Post-Standard "Deal With It" Jeanne Shenandoah December 13, 2006

Post-Standard "Spitzer seeks taxes on sales by tribes" Glenn Coin February 1, 2007

Post-Standard "Oneidas Hit The Jackpot" Glenn Coin February 7, 2007

Post-Standard "Disappearing Bees" editorial June 1, 2007

Empire Monthly "Honeybees Devastated by Mysterious Collapse" Brittney Fiorini Jerred June 2007

Post-Standard "Red and Black" Suzanne Baiz June 13, 2007

Post-Standard "Turning Stone Allowed To Continue Operating" Glenn Coin June 14, 2007

Post-Standard "Young Indians Rediscover...." Winnie Hu July 15, 2007

Post-Standard "Ley Creek-Without A Paddle" Delen Goldberg July 15, 2007

Post-Standard "LaFayette students can go online...." Elizabeth Doran July 23, 2007

Post-Standard "LaFayette to teach Onondaga language" Elizabeth Doran August 7, 2007

Post-Standard "A Historic Harvest" Scott Rapp August 20, 2008

OTHER ARTICLES:

"The Proclamation of 1763: Colonial Prelude To Two Centuries Of Federal-State Conflict Over The Management Of Indian Affairs" Boston University Law Review March 1989

"Children and Pesticides" U.S. Environmental Protection Agency 2003

"Honor Indian Treaties" Seneca Nation of Indians-Irving, NY 14081 2005

"Syracuse, New York-The Birthplace of American Democracy" September 16, 2005

"Indian Law Resource Center" Robert T. Coulter (self-published in Helena, MT) 2005

"Comments In Opposition To The Western Hemisphere Travel Initiative Requiring American Indians Traveling Into The United States From Canada To Carry A U.S. Or Canadian Passport" Robert Odawi Porter November 19, 2005

"Mitochondrial DNA 'clock' for the Amerinds and its implications for timing their entry into North America" Antonio Torroni, James V. Neel, Ramiro Barrantes, Theodore G. Schurr, and Douglas C. Wallace February, 1994

An Introduction to Archeology in Central New York" William M. Beauchamp Chapter N.Y.S.A.A. Vicky Jayne April 2005

Complaint for Declaratory Judgment: United States District Court-Northern District of New York (Onondaga Nation-plaintiff), (The State of New York-defendant) March 11, 2005

Nation to Nation Neighbors of the Onondaga Nation (NOON) 1999

Historical Timeline of *Haudenosaunee*-U.S. History (NOON) 1999
Sovereignty of the Onondaga Nation (NOON) 1999
Onondaga Nation Land Rights (NOON)
Indian Law Resource Center Helena, MT 2004
"Who Were The First Americans?" Michael D. Lemonick and Andrea
    Dorfman Time Magazine March 13, 2006
"What Ben Franklin didn't tell you about American Democracy" Donald A.
    Grinde, Jr. September 20, 2006
Land Rights Indian Law Resource Center Helena, MT 2008
"Warrior Road Trip" Canterbury Tours & Services Tunkhannock, PA 2008

PERSONAL LOAN: Brodhead, John Romeyn Esq. agent Documents
Relative to the Colonial History of the State of New York Procured in
Holland, England and France Weed, Parsons and Company, Printers
Albany, NY 1858 Transcripts of documents in the Royal Archives at the
Hague; in the Stad-Huys of the city of Amsterdam and in the Office of
the Secretary of State, Albany, New York.

My grateful thanks for the loan and research use of 3 out of all 9
volumes goes to Meg Bogosian, Manlius, NY.

Sylvester, Nathaniel Bartlett Northern New York and the Adirondack
Wilderness on loan from Jim Keebler, Pittsford, NY

Thanks also to Pat Ruggeri for the computer technology help and to
my wife, Michelle, for proofing my book.

I have to tell you that I hated doing term papers in high school and
college and that history was not my favorite subject either. This project was
started on March 21st of 2005 and culminated today, March 17th of 2008
with this 202 page book about a Nation that I have come to know all the
better. I have learned so much and I hope the same for you.

OTHERS: Lectures—Symposiums—Conferences—Interviews

> *"Vibrations of Conflict Leading People to Peaceful Resolutions:*
> *Don't Support People's Anger-Lead Them Out of It"*
> (Rainbow Weaver-Mohawk Healer)

The real story was told by:

Sid Hill, (Onondaga) *Tadodaho* of the Six Nations and, my quiet friend and a peacemaker. Listen and you will learn from this deep thinker.

Dr. Jack Rossen, Ithaca College 10/09/05

Dr. Robert Spiegelman, founder of Sullivanclinton.com, co-host (dedicated) 10/09/05

Birdie Hill (Cayuga), Heron Clan mother 10/09/05

Michael Acquilano, Staten Island Academy, historian 10/09/05

Dr. Geri Reisinger, (Seneca) Southern Door Project, Kingston/Wilkes-Barre 10/09/05

Kenn Anderson, Sr., historical tour developer for Sullivan-Clinton Campaign 10/09/05

Prof. Brook Olson, Share Farm-Cayuga 10/09/05

Robert Odawi Porter, (Seneca) Prof. of Law, and Director, Center for Indigenous Citizenship, Law, and Governance—Senior Associate Dean of Research Syracuse University College of Law, first Attorney General of the Seneca Nation, Chief Justice of the Sac and Fox Nation of Missouri, author of "Sovereignty, Colonialism, and The Indigenous Nations: A Reader" 10/4/05-11/19/05 (a very perceptive individual)

Carrie Garrow, (St. Regis Mohawk) Exec. Director of the Center for Indigenous Citizenship, Law, and Governance, Deputy District Attorney and Chief Judge of the St. Regis Mohawk Tribal Courts, co-author of "Tribal Criminal Law and Procedure" 11/19/05 (always a warm welcoming smile)

James Ransom, Chief of the St. Regis Mohawk Tribal Council 11/19/05

Brian Patterson, Men's Council of the Oneida Indian Nation 11/19/05 (good clear thoughts)

Richard E. Nephew, Council Chairperson of the Seneca Nation of Indians 11/19/05

Angie Barnes, Grand Chief, Mohawk Council of *Akwesasne*

Donald Maracle, Chief, Mohawks of the Bay of Quinte, *Tyendinaga* Mohawk Territory

Randy Phillips, Chief of the Oneida Nation of the Thames of Ontario 11/19/05

Jolene Rickard, PhD, panelist, writer, photographer State University of New York in Buffalo 11/08/05

Audra Simpson, PhD, Assistant Prof. of Anthropology at Cornell University 11/08/05

Chief Bradley Powless, Onondaga Nation Eel Clan 11/08/05

Taiaiake Alfred, (Mohawk), Indigenous Peoples Research Chair-University of Victoria, Author of "Heeding the Voices of Our Ancestors" and "Peace, Power, and Righteousness" and "*WASASE*-Indigenous Pathways of Action" 10/24/05 (really reaching out for peace)

Doug George Kanentiio, (Mohawk), another deep thinker 11/11/05

Freida Jacques, Onondaga Nation School 11/11/05, former Eel Clan mother, my friend, and teacher of the "accurate" past

Ed Running Fox, (Cherokee) sachem, physical and spiritual herbal healer (a most peaceful person) 11/11/05

Sandy Grande, Department Chair-Education Dept., Connecticut College, Author of "Red Pedagogy: Native American Social and Political Thought" 11/30/05

Dorothy Webster, Onondaga Eel Clan mother (wise, friendly, and most helpful)

Shirley Hill, Sports Director, *Tsha'Hon'nonyen'dakwa'* (Where They Play Games), my friend who loves lacrosse as much as I do, almost!)

Robert W. Venables, Cornell University American Indian Studies Program 4/11/06

Irving Powless, Jr. Chief of the Onondaga Nation Beaver Clan 4/11/06 (knowledge and wit)

Bea Gonzalez, President of the Syracuse Common Council, Dean of University College at Syracuse University (seeking social justice)

Wendy Gonyea, Onondaga Communications Office, *Haudenosaunee* Environmental Task Force, *Haudenosaunee* Standing Repatriation Committee, faith keeper, former teacher Onondaga Nation School, editor of the *Onondaga Nation News*, member of the Beaver Clan (very clear thoughts, a most peaceful personality)

There are others who have shared information and opinions with me but since they choose to remain anonymous, for whatever reason, I choose not to quote them since there is no reference back-up. There are politics on the rez and I don't intend to analyze the actions or words of different factions. I don't, and never will, live there so I can't speak with any authority. My opinions don't count for much.

GLOSSARY:

The Onondaga year begins in the Fall in traditional manner, so they start with:

October	*CHUTHOWAAH*	(little cold)
November	*CHUTHOWA*	(large cold)
December	*TISAH*	(little long day)
January	*TISGONAH*	(longer day)
February	*KANATOHA*	(winter leaves fall)
March	*KANATOGONAH*	(winter leaves fall and fill up the large hollows)
April	*ESUTAH*	(warm and good days)
May	*OYEAYEGONAH*	(leaves in full size, strawberries are ripe)
June	*SESKAHAH*	(sun goes for long days)
July	*SESKAGONAH*	(sun goes for longer days)
August	*KENTENAH*	(deer sheds its hair)
September	*KENTENAHGONAH*	(deer in its natural fur)

GONAH means something greater

Sunday	*AHWENTAHTOKENTE*	(holy day)
Monday	*AHWENTAHTENTAHEE*	(holy day over)
Tuesday	*TEKENWAHTONTAH*	(second one*)
Wednesday	*TAWENTOKEN*	(between the days)
Thursday	*KAHYEAYEWAHTONTAH*	(fourth one)
Friday	*WICKSWAHTONTAH*	(fifth one)
Saturday	*ENTUCKTAH*	(near the holy day)

* i.e. second day after Sunday

DNA (deoxyribonucleic acid)—the genetic substance that contains the information required to form a living creature.   (Sforza pg. 30)

European names:	Colonial equivalents:
War of the Grand Alliance (1689-1697)	King William's War
War of the Spanish Succession (1701-1714)	Queen Anne's War
War of the Austrian Succession (1740-1748)	King George's War
War of the Great Empire (1754-1763)	French and Indian War

(Bradfield pg. 14)

Printed in the United States
by Baker & Taylor Publisher Services